Christmas
by the
Lighthouse

Christmas
by the
Lighthouse

REBECCA BOXALL

LAKE UNION
PUBLISHING

Text copyright © 2019 by Rebecca Boxall

Published by Lake Union Publishing, Seattle

www.apub.com

Amazon, the Amazon logo, and Lake Union Publishing are trademarks of Amazon.com, Inc., or its affiliates.

ISBN-13: 9781542009614
ISBN-10: 1542009618

Cover design by Lisa Horton

Printed in the United States of America

In memory of Prinny (1981–1990)
And for my family – Dan, Ruby, Iris and Joey

PART ONE

Falling

April–May 2017

Chapter One

Jersey, Tuesday

Jude

He was alive, but he wasn't living.

He was thirty-six years old and he'd never even been in love, for goodness' sake! Still, he had a decent job – which he was determined to be grateful for, given the perilous state of the economy. Never mind that it bored him to tears.

Jude was trained as a teacher but for the last four years he'd worked as a call centre operative for the international banking arm of Hedgeleys Bank, where he sat all day long dealing with calls from unhappy customers. Or, if he was lucky, from clients who couldn't be bothered to check their account balances online so who called him up instead. He felt his soul being destroyed with every day that passed.

His colleague Derek, who'd sat in the pod next to him until recently, had clearly felt the same. He went out to get a sandwich one lunch break, leaving his jacket behind on his chair, and never returned. Jude envied Derek. He'd told his sister, Daisy, all about it the day it happened, calling her just before she started her shift at St Thomas's Hospital in London.

'Why do you envy him?' she'd asked. 'Jude, what the hell's the poor sod going to do now? He won't get a reference, will he? *And* he'll have to buy a new jacket.' Daisy was always one to consider practicalities.

'I suppose I just admire anyone who has the gumption to actually do something to change their life if it isn't working for them.'

'Come on, Jude. There's loads you could do to change things if you really wanted to. You could join an online dating agency, find a new job. Why not rent an apartment by the sea instead of *mouldering* in that grubby little basement flat in town?'

Jude laughed. Daisy had a knack for using particularly descriptive words, emphasising them in her naturally dramatic way. 'Mouldering' was a definite Daisy word.

And it was true; he could do all of those things. In an island with some of the world's most beautiful beaches, it made no sense to be living where he did with an urban view of St Helier's rusting cylindrical gasholder.

But he just didn't have the energy to change. Perhaps he was depressed? But didn't that mean you couldn't even get out of bed? He *always* got out of bed eventually. He religiously kicked off his duvet after pressing his 'snooze' button three times, then took a deep breath before hauling himself into the shower, listening to Chris Evans's breakfast show. This always perked him up a little but he definitely wasn't one to whistle or sing in the shower. Instead he tended to bow his head, resigning himself to the day ahead and letting the water pour over him, into his eyes and down his body, until his allotted five minutes of hot water ran out and he was forced to search around blindly for his towel, put in his contact lenses and, shivering, run to his bedroom to dress.

The fact he'd never been in love was at the top of his list of personal failings. It was something he was deeply ashamed of, suspecting it indicated a significant flaw in either his looks or his personality. Actually, he thought it must be the latter (surely worse than unfortunate looks) as his friends had told him that, of all of them, he was the one who attracted women on a night out. The rest of his mates would take full advantage of this, while by the end of the night it would be Jude propping up the bar alone, staring into his drink.

On this particular Tuesday morning, having now showered and dressed in his Marks and Spencer's suit, he checked himself in the hall mirror before leaving the flat. He tried to view himself objectively. Tall, for a start. That was considered an advantage on the whole. Hair once described as 'tousled and golden' by an ex, though he deemed it messy and dark blonde. Chameleon eyes that were green or blue, depending on his surroundings, with long lashes that by some stroke of luck were dark despite his fair hair. A square jaw sporting 'designer' stubble (laziness when it came to shaving). Slim, though not very muscly – again, too lazy. He really should take some exercise. But overall not *too* bad, all things considered.

He grabbed his umbrella and locked the front door behind him, ruminating on the shortcomings of his personality on his fifteen-minute walk through the rain-lashed streets of St Helier to the office. After all, a little critical self-talk was just the sort of start to their day a possibly depressed person needed.

He was lazy. He was directionless. He was boring. This last self-criticism horrified him the most. *Was* he boring? He certainly led a dull life, but did this make him dreary as a person as well? He would have to ask his friends. But hang on, no – that would just add another couple of unattractive characteristics to his growing list: needy and insecure.

Having set himself up for the day with such turgid introspection, Jude arrived at the bank. He'd decided that Tuesdays were even worse than Mondays. At least Mondays offered the chance to chat with colleagues about the weekend. Okay, so in his case this was unlikely to be a riveting conversation, principally centring on what he'd watched on Netflix, but it allowed for a little light banter by the photocopier. By Tuesday, though, the weekend was dealt with and no one in their right mind would be optimistic enough to discuss plans for the following one.

He entered the open-plan office, sighed, and switched on his computer – blanching at the white light that had started to give him headaches – then waited twitchily until he could log in and set himself up with his headset, ready for the first call of the day. Then he checked his watch. He had seven minutes – just enough time to get himself a hot drink.

But before he'd managed to take one step away from his desk he found himself blockaded by Helena from two pods down, who pressed an envelope into his hands while she stuffed down a chocolate muffin, heedless of the crumbs she was leaving to fester on the carpet beneath his desk. She was looking particularly hard done by today.

'Jude, can I have a word?' she asked, looking shiftily from left to right. Then, not waiting for Jude to answer, she continued. 'It's Peggy,' she whispered. 'I said to her yesterday, I haven't had an appraisal in three years. *Three years*. It's an abomination. The appraisal policy clearly states that everyone should get one on an annual basis. Have you had one?' she asked, clearly suspecting herself of being singled out as a victim of this management failure.

Jude thought about their manager, Peggy. She was a complete workaholic and a terrible stickler for the rules, but Jude had nurtured a soft spot for her ever since she'd given him the job in the bank at a time when he'd been in no fit state to be offered a position anywhere. 'Er, no,' Jude replied. 'But I'm not that fussed really . . .'

'Not fussed? This is your career!' Helena told him, unable to maintain her whisper in her indignation. 'Your career! And you're not *fussed*? It's that kind of passive behaviour that management relies on to get away with their continued scandalous conduct.'

Abandoning the envelope on his desk, Jude began to edge around Helena, still hopeful for a coffee, but she was not so easily deterred. As he snuck past her, towards the corridor, she abandoned her muffin and followed him. Jude wondered if she was actually going to stalk him all the way to the kitchen but he soon realised, with relief, that Helena had spotted Peggy arriving for the day.

She was walking into her office when Jude saw her clock Helena stomping towards her: the poor woman looked like a rabbit caught in the headlights and, despite her numerous shortcomings, Jude couldn't help feeling sorry for her. He checked his watch again. Only two minutes to go. He'd have to forgo his coffee.

Back at his desk he picked up the envelope Helena had left with him and spotted the note attached to it asking for a cash contribution and his signature on the greetings card within. He opened it. *You're having a baby!* the front of the card screamed, stating the bleeding obvious to whoever the recipient was. He wondered who it might be. He checked inside. Ann.

'Who's Ann?' Jude asked Suki, Derek's recent replacement, who'd just arrived for the day and was in the process of logging in. She'd only been working there two weeks but she seemed to know who Ann was instantly. She flicked back her mane of glossy black hair, parted in the middle and clearly influenced by the Kardashian sisters, and stared at him through enormous Deirdre Barlow glasses (so geeky he assumed they must be cool).

'Dur! *Ann*, of course!'

This wasn't particularly helpful. Suki was fresh out of university ('uni', as she called it) and seemed remarkably stupid considering she'd come away with first-class honours. Jude thought it must be an enormous effort to come across as so ditzy when she was actually extremely clever. She was on the management trainee programme and hadn't been there long enough to lose faith in being 'fast-tracked'. Jude had been promised the same when he'd started four years before, though he'd cared very little then and was certainly past caring now.

'I don't know anyone called Ann! She's not on this floor, is she?'

'Er, like, yeah! She's the one with, like, the fat belly? Waddles around, moaning about her back? One of the client managers?' Every statement was a question as far as Suki was concerned.

Jude literally didn't know who Ann was, and the office wasn't even very big, but he decided to save face.

'Oh *yeah*! Of course,' he replied. Oh well. He wrote along his usual lines: *Dear Ann, Congratulations! All the best, Jude.* He got so bored of writing 'Congratulations!' in these cards that he'd once used his thesaurus to look for another expression. But 'Whoopee doo' sounded slightly sarcastic so he'd stuck to boring old 'Congratulations!' Most of the time, if he knew the person, he was genuinely pleased for them. But he couldn't help but wonder when it would be *his* turn. Surely one day he'd be on the receiving end of a 'Congratulations!' for something or other: getting engaged, tying the knot, fathering a baby, passing some more exams, having another baby. The only one that seemed inevitable was retirement, but that was still a long way off and he didn't want to accelerate the ageing process, no matter how keenly he desired a Hallmark card signed by a floor-full of reluctant colleagues.

At the end of the day, having achieved very little, Jude plodded home. He ate beans on toast, watched a series of tedious TV programmes and was in bed by nine. *What the hell is happening to me?* he wondered, as he drifted off to sleep. When exactly had his life come to this?

Chapter Two

ENGLAND, TUESDAY

SUMMER

'Can you see my glasses anywhere?' asked Summer, groping around on the bedside table. She screwed up her bright-blue eyes but it was no good; she couldn't see a thing.

Seth rummaged around on the duvet between them and passed her the dark-framed glasses.

'You always just leave them in the middle of the bed when you conk out,' he complained. 'One of these nights I'll squash them when I roll over.' Seth picked up the romance novel Summer had also left in the centre of the bed and inspected it with a grimace. 'Never judge a book by its cover, I suppose,' he remarked as he passed it to Summer rather gingerly, as though concerned his superior intellect might be contaminated just by touching the thing.

'Thanks,' she smiled, ignoring Seth's scathing remark about her perfectly acceptable reading material and plonking the glasses on to her nose. They were a little smeared, but she could see a lot better than without them. She pushed back her dark hair and jumped out of bed.

'What's your day looking like?' Seth asked next, as he pulled himself up in the bed and watched Summer dress. She preferred a nightly bath to a morning shower, so she always got ready for the day immediately. She searched around for her 'uniform', as she thought of it – the kind of clothes she found dreadfully dreary but which she'd learnt were considered acceptable for a headmaster's wife. She pulled on a stripy blue-and-white T-shirt, a navy cardigan and some dark denim jeans, then made her way through to the bathroom to put in her contact lenses and wash her face.

'I have to file an article by lunchtime,' she called back to the bedroom. 'Then it's the Tuesday Group at one and I've promised to take a pudding. I opted for Eton Mess. Surely even I can't cock that up?'

'But you hate Tuesday Group.'

'Of course I do. I hate most of the things expected of me as a headmaster's wife but – angel that I am – I do them all anyway.' She poked her head back round the bedroom door with a smile.

'I don't deserve you,' said Seth, with a rather heavy sigh.

'Probably not,' Summer agreed light-heartedly, though she paused and looked at her husband as he sat frowning on the bed. She could remember falling for him as if it were yesterday – attracted by the gravitas he seemed to exude. Summer had loved her hippy childhood but there had been a gap that hadn't been filled until she'd met Seth – that funny dweeb of a boy fresh from boarding school, on his gap year before heading out into the world.

Seth had told Summer later that when they'd met that fateful day, when he'd spotted her at the side of the road after her orange camper van had broken down, he'd never even kissed a girl before! And there Summer had been, with her hippy clothes and carefree smile, a whole world of experience behind her despite the fact she was almost two years younger than him.

Seth had always maintained that he'd fallen in love with her in the blink of an eye and she'd often wondered if he'd regretted committing to someone so different from him, though he'd always stuck by his 'opposites attract' cliché. For Summer, falling for Seth had been a slightly slower process. Seth had helped her tow the van to the nearest garage and he'd pressed her for her phone number, though she hadn't made it easy for him.

'Can I get your number?' he asked.

'I don't have a phone, I'm afraid,' Summer replied.

'Well, your address then?' Seth tried.

'I'm kind of here, there and everywhere,' Summer explained, then she realised she was probably putting him off when she didn't necessarily want to. He wasn't her type at all, but he had lovely dark looks and an earnest expression that was rather appealing.

'Look,' Summer said, 'I drink at the pub down by the river quite a bit – you know, the Cuckoo? Maybe I'll see you there some time. I definitely owe you a drink. You've been amazing! Goodbye, serious boy,' she said, laughing at him gently. And she'd kissed him on the lips, just like that.

Seth had been hooked and had gone to the Cuckoo every night for two weeks, his doggedness finally paying off. Summer had been there with a group of friends, daringly drinking alcohol even though she was only seventeen. When she'd seen him turn up in the pub and realised how much effort he'd put into finding her, she'd been charmed. After that, it hadn't taken long for her to become as smitten as him.

Now, Summer turned from the door and made her way along the hallway with a view to FaceTiming their boys: the twins she'd become pregnant with the very first time she and Seth had gone to bed together. She'd sometimes considered whether the many contrasts in their personalities might have put an end to their relationship early on if it hadn't been for that accidental pregnancy.

Summer sighed, but then cheered up again as she fiddled around with the iPad and dialled Levi's number. The FaceTiming was a weekly arrangement and was far too early as far as the boys were concerned, so she barely got anything out of them. But it was easier than trying to catch them in the evening – their social life was rampant. Her twins were twenty and in their second year at the same university where they studied the same course and lived in the same house, even though, like Summer and Seth, they were very different characters – Luke a happy-go-lucky sort for whom the phrase 'winging it' might have been invented, and Levi a planner who left nothing to chance. But they were the best of friends, which, whenever Summer thought about it, gave her a warm glow. If she'd done nothing else right in her life, she felt she'd at least brought up two very lovely boys.

'Morning, whippersnappers,' she said as she peered at the screen. Luke and Levi sat side by side, yawning, mugs of coffee in their hands. Identical to look at, they were also pretty much replicas of their mother, with unruly dark hair, piercing blue eyes and – except at this time of the morning – beaming smiles. Their features weren't as delicate as Summer's, though, who had what she'd been told was a 'pixie' (or sometimes plain old 'naughty') face thanks to her tiny nose and dimpled chin and cheeks.

Seth had been dark like her and the boys, though his hair was quickly becoming 'salt-and-pepper' as he approached forty, and his eyes were much more serious. He probably had the most engaging smile of all of them but he was less forthcoming with his. In some ways, it made the smile all the more enchanting when it finally arrived, like being paid a compliment by someone who has impossibly high standards.

Having dragged some news out of the twins, Summer switched off FaceTime and turned to the BBC website, searching for a recipe for Eton Mess. Before starting to gather ingredients, she read it through twice – a discipline she'd come to realise was essential to implement, for she suffered from what she called 'recipe dyslexia', always missing some crucial component or instruction, which had led to some fairly unappetising meals over the years. Despite that, she never ran out of optimism when it came to cooking; always convinced that – somewhere inside her – a fantastic chef was lurking and, if she just kept on trying, it would eventually emerge.

The Mess finally concocted, she slotted it into the fridge and found her fluorescent sticky notes. She scribbled on two of them *Remember pudding!* and placed one on the fridge and the other on the front door, a nifty trick she'd learnt to help with her uncooperative memory. She checked her watch. Her deadline was one o'clock and the article she was due to file needed an awful lot of polishing. She abandoned the muddle in the kitchen and hurried through to the study, where she found her laptop and went to open the article.

'Where is it?' she asked herself. She searched. A sinking sensation was swiftly followed by a slightly sick feeling. After a panicky five minutes, it was clear the document was gone. She hadn't saved it. A computer whizz-kid might well have been able to retrieve it from some cloud or other but sadly she was no expert and she hadn't the time to locate one. Seth was even worse than her at computers. There was no other option – she'd have to rewrite it. She racked her brain, trying to remember what she'd written on the subject of 'Sexual Positions in your Thirties', as the article was called. Ironic, really, considering she and Seth hadn't had sex for nearly a year.

She was, to the horror of several of the school parents, a journalist for the 'women's health' section of a well-known magazine. When she'd taken the job, she'd expected to be researching articles on fad diets and revolutionary vitamins, but by and large the editor, Guy Simmons (a man Summer had decided was a complete pervert), wanted Summer to write about sex. By twelve forty-five she'd emailed her hastily invented article to Guy, fingers and toes crossed it wouldn't bring about a most unpleasant rage (he was fiery as well as perverted), then dashed back to the kitchen.

She started gathering her jacket, handbag and keys, all the while muttering *Eton Mess, Eton Mess, Eton Mess* to herself. She got a little flustered when she couldn't find her ballet pumps but, eventually ready, she raced out of the door and drove as fast as she could within the village speed limits to Barbara Robinson's house, where today's Tuesday Group – a gathering of middle-aged women with connections to the school – was to take place. She slammed the car door, made her way up Barbara's front path and rang the bell.

'Hello!' welcomed Barbara, who leant forward, reeking of Chanel No. 5, all set for some air kissing. But Summer stood stock still as, for the second time that day, her stomach lurched.

She'd forgotten the bloody Eton Mess.

Chapter Three

JERSEY, THURSDAY

JUDE

Thursday morning and he tramped through the side door of the bank and deliberated over whether to take the lift or the stairs. Taking the lift was like a game of Russian roulette – half the time it gave out on the way up to the third floor – but Jude wasn't sure he could face three flights of stairs at this time in the morning. He felt headachy and fatigued. Then again, it would be good exercise, would set him up nicely for the day. In fact, he could eat the pastry he'd just bought without feeling guilty. Jude wavered.

He took the lift.

It was his lucky day. Amazingly, he made it all the way up without incident. Today he'd decided to bring coffee in with him. He didn't want a repeat of Tuesday's performance when Helena had thwarted his coffee-making attempts. He checked his watch. Four minutes until the first call. He scrolled down his emails, deleting several trivial-looking items without reading them (*Has anyone seen my mug?* and *Important training session*), then let out a tut of frustration. There was one from his mum. He must have told her a million times not to email him at work but to his personal address instead, explaining about the bank's resident IT geek who made no secret of the fact that he got all his kicks from reading employees' personal correspondence. But Beryl was not very tech-savvy and clearly hadn't worked out how to remove Jude's work email address from her list of default contacts. Jude opened it.

G'day from Australia, it began, as her emails always did. *How are you? Hope work isn't too stressful. Is that boss of yours being a cow? And do you think she's still having it off with that chap from IT?*

Jude groaned.

Everything's fine here in Perth. It's autumn now so the days aren't so hot – a relief for us Brits. Still mid-twenties and sunny most days. I've joined a new bridge club – a good bunch of people although the woman who hosts it can be a bit snotty. I always thought you wouldn't get snobs in Australia but I guess they get everywhere. Dad is doing okay after his hip op – walking around now and in a lot less pain. Have you heard from Daisy? She seems to have gone 'off grid'.

Jude snorted at his mum's use of the expression. She sounded like an undercover agent. Too many Aussie cop shows.

Love to you, as always. Come and stay soon. Love Mum x

Nowadays, thinking about his mum caused Jude very normal conflicting feelings of affection and irritation. For the first couple of months after his parents had emigrated, if he'd thought about his mother at all he'd wanted to howl like a two-year-old. He'd been eighteen.

Jude had been mollycoddled as a baby and all through his childhood. He was a shy child, gawky and four-eyed, his only saving grace a natural ability at games that – by and large – prevented him from suffering a school lifetime of bullying at the boys-only secondary he attended in Jersey. As it was, he was neither popular nor (save for one small period in his life) one of the poor dweebs who regularly suffered the merciless ridiculing of the cool boys. He seemed generally to blend pretty much into the background, a position he was more than happy to live with. And home life, by contrast, was blissful. A cosy mother – blonde, nurturing and happily domesticated – and a steady, breadwinning father who stood dutifully at the sidelines and cheered when Jude managed to get into the Under Fifteens rugby team. Daisy, his bossy older sister, was a little on the jealous side, having decided that Jude was her parents' favourite, but she was still grudgingly loving and caring – particularly about Jude's rugby injuries. She loved a bit of blood and gore.

Jude imagined his life would continue like this, a life where, whatever the outside world threw at him, home – the home he'd lived in his entire life in the seaside parish of St Brelade – would always be there, reassuringly dated in its decor but smelling perpetually of Mum's dinners and freshly ironed laundry. A place where his mother would be ready at the door to welcome him with her sweetly perfumed kisses and his father would pat him on the back and be ready with a listening ear.

But he was wrong. Unbeknown to him, his parents had always planned to move to Australia, where his mother's sister – Auntie Irene – had lived since marrying an Aussie at the age of twenty-one. And, loving though she was, Beryl believed that a child miraculously turned into an adult the minute their eighteenth birthday arrived. So when that time came, while her affection towards Jude had not diminished exactly, it had altered sufficiently to enable her to make the decision. She and Jude's father put the family home on the market. They were going to Australia. The news came a fortnight after Jude found out he'd got into Exeter University to train as a teacher. Having imagined he would return at the end of every term to the cosy bosom of his family, he was devastated.

Of course, his parents offered for both Jude and Daisy to emigrate with them. For Daisy, it was clear-cut. She was two years into training as a doctor at King's in London and was not quite so tied to Beryl's apron strings as Jude. She would visit, she promised them, but she wouldn't move. Jude, on the other hand, didn't know what to do. It was a big enough change for him to be moving to England after eighteen years solid on the tiny island of Jersey, but Australia? In all honesty, he didn't fancy it. He dithered for weeks, unable to decide, until in the end his father told him what he thought Jude should do.

'Get your studies done in the UK,' said his dad. 'Then, when those years are done, come to Australia and be with us then. I'm sure you'll be able to convert your qualification easily enough so you can teach in Perth. And we'll be there, welcoming you with open arms, a few years down the line.'

Jude had taken his father's advice, but he'd been a mess – unable to enjoy his first term at university, feeling embarrassingly sorry for himself about it all, with his misery heightened by all the frolics going on around him as the freshers became legless and played practical jokes on each other.

Ultimately, however, he'd got over it and had joined in the partying and the studying. And he'd somehow never gone to join his parents in the end, though he'd holidayed with them over several Christmases – the happy cliché of a barbie on the beach. Instead, he'd returned to Jersey, rented himself a flat and taken up his first teaching job, a career he'd achieved a huge amount of satisfaction from until that fateful day.

It had been Jude's thirty-second birthday and he'd spent it dealing mainly, as usual, with his delinquent student – a sixteen-year-old called Melvin with a number of issues. School had finished for the day and Jude had decided to get his marking done there, rather than in the comfort of his own home – a decision he would come to regret. He'd turned the classroom lights off and headed down the corridor, out the front doors and along the pathway that led to the car park. He'd seen a boy in a hoody, just along the path from him, spraying graffiti on the wall.

'Hey! Stop that! Hey, you!' he'd bellowed at the figure. The boy had turned and run and, with some kind of misguided heroic instinct, Jude had run after him. He would never have caught up with him, but the boy had tripped and fallen, quickly getting to his feet just as Jude reached him.

'Melvin!' he'd shouted, realising now who the culprit was. 'You're going to be in big trouble for this. Just you wait until . . .' The remaining words had been taken from him as a sharp pain overwhelmed him. He'd reached for his stomach and felt the blood oozing from it. He'd been stabbed – the knife narrowly missing a major artery.

Jude had survived. But something had happened to him that evening. He felt utterly pathetic about it, but the whole experience had robbed him of his already shaky self-confidence. He'd carried on teaching for a short while, once he'd physically recovered, but he'd lost his enthusiasm for it, and after a couple of months he'd handed in his notice and found himself his safe yet soul-destroying job at Hedgeleys.

But Jude realised when enough was enough. One way or another, he had to at least *try* to grapple his way out of this beige existence that had, somewhere along the lines, become his own.

Chapter Four

England, Thursday

Summer

The bungalow was, on the face of it, both neat and homely. Summer always just hoped fervently no visitor would think to open any cupboards, where her true slovenly nature won out – to the despair of Seth, who often grumbled about being the victim of Summer's cruel practical jokes when he opened a cupboard door only to have the entire contents fall on top of him, usually prompting him to mutter something about how *it never rains but it pours* if he was in a bad mood or there being *no point in crying over spilt milk* if he was in a more forgiving one. Summer sometimes thought he was just a walking cliché.

Just as she tried to conform with her own outward appearance, so Summer did her best to keep 'Headmaster's House', as it was known, clean and tidy. The place was not owned by them but was theirs for the taking all the while Seth was headmaster of Camford Preparatory School (so far, ten years) on the outskirts of the village of Camford, near Peterborough. The school was an imposing Victorian building with several classroom Portakabins and the head's modern bungalow hidden discreetly behind it.

Summer had her methods to help her in this quest for tidiness. Music mainly. Radio 2 was her favourite, especially Chris Evans's breakfast show, and she found that if she danced her way around the house the chores weren't *quite* as boring. It was the futility of it all that annoyed her. What was the point of cleaning and tidying when it didn't last longer than a day? But then perhaps that could be said of lots of things. She just wished she were more of a natural at it. Her friend Tilly was exceptionally neat and Summer observed her when she was round having coffee, making a mental note of the way she went about things. Summer and Tilly had been friends for ten years – ever since Seth had become headmaster at Camford. She'd been the first person to drop round, a dish of lasagne in her hands. Summer was a pescatarian, but she'd been hugely appreciative of the gesture, and she'd known that Seth, an enthusiastic meat-eater, would be thrilled.

'Welcome to the village!' Tilly had beamed. Summer had invited her into the bungalow and Tilly had placed the carefully cling-filmed dish down on the kitchen top and turned to embrace Summer in a hug, as if she were simply a friend she hadn't seen in years rather than someone she'd never met before.

Tilly was a warm person, always full of compliments, but there was just one part of her character that over the years Summer had learnt to be cautious about. Tilly was a *tiny* bit controlling. She had exceptionally high expectations and at times Summer felt her failure to match up to them frustrated her friend. Still, being a control freak had its advantages – Tilly's enormous house at the centre of the village was always pristine, and Summer had realised that it wasn't even that much of an effort for Tilly to keep it that way. It was completely natural for her to take a pan out of a cupboard, use it, wash it up and pop it straight back, when Summer would have just left the pan to soak in the sink.

Summer's other weak point was organisation. Oh, how she tried! She wasn't one of those people who laughed indulgently at their own chaos while clearly considering themselves charmingly unconventional.

She really, really wanted to be organised. She'd tried everything over the years to remember birthdays, school events when the boys were little, obligations associated with her own and Seth's jobs and social functions. But the bottom line was that she was hopeless, and no whiteboard or cleverly reminding mobile phone could entirely transform her. Seth put it down to her upbringing, which had been severely lacking in structure and discipline, even if it had been rather lovely.

Summer's latest organisational test was Seth's fortieth. Encouraged by Tilly, she'd arranged a surprise party.

'Seth's not even much of a party person!' Summer had argued with her friend.

'But you've got to do something!' Tilly had said as she towel-dried her hair. They'd just been for a swim at their local gym.

'But couldn't I just do a family meal or something?'

'Come on, Summer. That's a cop-out. It's his fortieth. He'll be expecting something.'

'Yes, of course he will. And quite rightly, too . . . A surprise party, you think?'

'Perfect. I'll help. Come to mine for coffee now and we'll get everything organised. I'm happy to make the cake.'

'Oh, would you?' Summer had asked gratefully. She hated baking.

And so she'd sent out invitations to all their friends and had ordered a job lot of tacky fortieth decorations from the 'Part-eee Shop'. Seth was very particular about alcohol so she'd contacted the twins for advice – a barrel of real ale, Nyetimber sparkling wine and a robust red like a Shiraz, apparently. The boys promised to be there for the do, though the rest of their Easter holidays would be spent inter-railing through Europe. Food-wise, Summer couldn't quite afford caterers but she and Tilly had decided to make a vast array of salads, quiches and sandwiches and she planned to buy a selection of canapés and crudités from M&S.

She'd wondered about holding the party in the back garden but April was a funny time of year so she'd plumped for the school dining room in the end. At least it was available, being the Easter holidays, and all the tables, chairs, glasses and crockery they could need would be to hand.

Now it was the day before the party, and Summer felt quite frazzled as thoughtless guests rang to back out at the last minute or finally answered their invitations, saying they were coming after all when Summer had counted them out. It was early evening and a beautiful one. Cool, but the sky was dusky pink and she took a beer through to the conservatory where she sat in near darkness and allowed the alcohol and the outside scene to soothe her frayed nerves. She rubbed her knotty shoulders and closed her eyes, then opened them again as she heard Seth pad into the room.

'Summer,' he said. He sounded strange. Not quite like himself.

She patted the seat beside her. 'Come and join me,' she said. But he didn't. He remained standing, still dressed in formal clothing despite the time of day. Seth took great pride in looking smart at all times.

'Summer, I need to talk to you . . .'

'Okay,' Summer smiled. 'What is it?'

'Well, the thing is . . . How to say this . . . Summer, I . . .' He cleared his throat. 'Summer, I want a break.'

'A holiday? We're going to book Provence next week, aren't we?'

'No, not a holiday. A break from our marriage. I'm so sorry,' he said, tears in his eyes, and Summer was amazed. He must be feeling anguished, as she'd never once seen him cry. 'I've been thinking about it for weeks. Maybe it's a midlife crisis . . . turning forty . . . I just feel like I'm suffocating. I'm sorry. It's not you, it's me,' he said, and Summer's first thought was that it was so typically clichéd of him to say that.

The initial irritation then made way for shock. Admittedly their relationship had been a bit strained over the last year, the intimate side in particular having gone downhill, but Summer hadn't seen this coming – it was, as Seth would say, a complete bolt from the blue. Tears sprung to her own eyes. She felt hurt and cold and shivery.

'Why a break? If you're that unhappy with me, why not finish things completely?' she asked, wiping tears away on her jumper sleeve.

'No, no, no – I don't want that, not at all . . . I just need some time apart – six months, say . . . a bit of space. At this moment in time I'm not sure I'm worth being around.'

Summer was utterly confused. 'But *why*, Seth? What's going on? Is it something I've done?'

'No! I don't know. I'm so sorry . . . It's just a need. A strong urge for some time alone.'

Seth had never been much of a talker and Summer resigned herself to the fact that she wouldn't be able to get a proper explanation out of him. And did it really matter? Whatever the reason, he was quietly adamant.

Eventually, feeling drained, Summer went to bed. She was slightly surprised when Seth got in beside her. She lay there, her mind whirring as Seth began to grind his teeth in his sleep. As she fidgeted wake-fully, dozens of thoughts ran through her head, leaving her feeling sad, rejected, stunned and . . . What was the other feeling, lying just beneath the surface and yet quite keen to be identified? It took Summer a moment to realise it was *relief*. A six-month break. The shocking request, turned on its head, was perhaps not a wholly unpleasant pros-pect. Six months of freedom, of opportunity. A break from a life that she knew, in her heart, she'd never been truly suited to living. For a moment, Summer felt guilty about such thoughts, but not for long. After all, none of it was her idea.

The party the following day was a surprising success, considering Seth's revelation the night before. Luke and Levi arrived in the morning and helped Summer get everything ready, with the assistance of the highly organised Tilly. The dining hall began to look festive. Seth went off to play golf but, having strict instructions to be home for a birthday lunch, he arrived back by midday and spruced himself up, dressing in his favourite chinos, blazer and penny loafers. He was staggered when he was dragged across to the dining hall and there came upon his extended family and many old and new friends. He looked like he might burst into tears when he saw what Summer had arranged for him. Tears under control, he then looked incredibly guilty – the epitome of shame-faced. Summer actually felt quite sorry for him.

After lunch, and with everyone rather merry, Summer was approached by Luke. 'Mum, do you think we should get Dad to do a speech?'

'Oh, I don't know . . .' Summer began, thinking it might be terribly awkward for him in the circumstances, which were only known to him and Summer at this stage. But Tilly had overheard.

'Of course he must give a little speech!' she said. 'All these people have come from far and wide. Well, one of you should anyway. Or the boys?'

Luke instantly blushed. If there was one thing her twins hated it was to be the centre of attention, a sentiment Summer shared. Seth, on the other hand, was used to public speaking as a headmaster, though she wondered what on earth he would say. A small part of her (the rejected part) wanted to put him on the spot, to make him sweat. She found him chatting to an old university pal.

'Excuse me,' she said, interrupting. 'I'm so sorry, Paul, do you mind if I steal Seth away for a moment?'

'Not at all, darling Summer. But come and find me in a minute so we can have a good old catch-up.'

'Will do, I promise,' she said, and Paul discreetly disappeared.

'Summer, I don't know what to say,' Seth began. 'I feel so bad. I had no idea you were planning all this, or I'd have . . .'

'What? Never suggested a break?' Summer asked archly.

'I . . . I don't know. I mean, I just feel bad.'

Summer softened. 'I know. Look, Tilly thinks you should make a brief speech, thank everyone for coming. Would you mind?'

'I probably should, she's right,' he agreed, though it must have been galling to admit it – Seth and Tilly had never seen eye to eye. 'Give me five minutes.'

As promised, five minutes later Seth tapped on his glass with a fork. Gradually, the hum of conversation died down and he began.

'I just wanted to say a few words, if you can bear it,' he announced, with a slight laugh. 'Firstly, an enormous thank you to all of you who've made the effort today to travel here and celebrate the fact that I am now *officially* old. Some of you might say I've been old since the day I was born and, I'm sorry to admit, you clearly know me far too well.' There was a titter among the revellers. 'A little joke, anyway, from serious old me. I must also thank my lovely boys. They'll be squirming now. Where are they? Ah yes, I can see them trying to hide. And then, of course, there's Summer. We're very different people, as you'll all be aware, but somehow or other we've made things work. Summer's strongest asset is her patience. And right now, I know I'm really testing that. Thank you, Summer. For bearing with me.'

Summer wiped away a tear.

'What's all that about?' asked Tilly, and Summer smiled bravely.

'I'll tell you later,' she said above the chatter and applause. She shook her head, and the tears receded. 'Now, come on, let's do the cake.'

The party over, the following day there were practicalities to be considered, and these had never been Summer's forte. Both feeling a little hungover – the party having gone on into the evening – Seth and Summer looked at each other despondently across the kitchen table. They'd woken up the boys so that they could share their sorry news with them first.

'What's going on?' asked Levi, always keen to have mysteries solved as quickly as possible. Summer looked towards Seth.

'I'm sorry. There's no easy way to say this. It's just that Mum and I are going to have a little break from each other . . . some time off from our marriage. We wanted to tell you both first, before we set anything practical in motion.'

Luke looked shocked. 'A break? A marital holiday?' he said, almost laughing. 'I'm not sure marriage is meant to work like that!'

'It's quite common nowadays,' Seth persevered, and Summer found herself quite enjoying watching him squirm, though she planned to back him up when the boys inevitably asked her about it.

Levi looked at her. 'Do you both want this break?' he asked. 'Or is this all just Dad's idea?' Levi had always been particularly protective of Summer.

'It was Dad's *idea*,' Summer said carefully. 'But having thought about it, I think it's a good suggestion. A little breather might be healthy for us!'

Seth looked at her. He seemed surprised, though relieved.

'If you're sure?' Levi asked, frowning.

'Yes, I'm sure – I promise. We've been together a long time and every marriage has its ups and downs. Hopefully in six months' time we can all get back to normal. I'm sorry, though, to spring this on you.' Summer took a breath. 'Now, Dad and I have to talk about all the boring practicalities, so you can go back to bed if you want?'

Luke shrugged. 'It could be worse,' he said philosophically. 'You could be splitting up for good.' Both boys gave Summer a hug and then sloped off back to their bedrooms.

'I feel awful,' Seth remarked, and Summer found her patience starting to wane.

'I suppose we should talk about what we're going to do. How it's going to work? Do you want to move out, or shall I?'

'I'm so sorry, *again*, but I have to stay here. It's part of the deal with the school. The head must be in residence within the grounds.'

'Of course, I'm not thinking straight. So I need to be the one to move out.'

'I feel dreadful.'

'Don't, Seth, I can't keep reassuring you. It's what you want. And now that I've got over the shock, I'm okay with the idea. It's an adventure and my life's been slim on adventure for a while. There's just one thing, Seth. If anything major happens to do with the boys, we should contact each other. But aside from that I'd prefer it if we didn't speak or text or anything. Is that okay?' Seth nodded, clearly in agreement. 'Good. Well, I'll give Tilly a call later to explain. See what she suggests about my living arrangements.'

Seth frowned, no doubt thinking that Tilly's place might be a bit too close for comfort. Tilly would almost certainly offer for Summer to move into her huge house with her – her husband was about to undertake some kind of advanced pilot training in America and both children were at boarding school, so she'd probably enjoy the company – but Summer wasn't sure she wanted to remain nearby herself. If they were to have a break, it needed to be a proper one. And her 'no contact' rule would be seriously tested if she were to stay at Tilly's.

Later, she found her address book and flicked through it. A, B, C, D . . . De la Haye, Sylvie. Of course! Her Aunt Sylvie. Her mother's sister. She lived miles away, in Jersey, and always enjoyed company. She would try Sylvie. Summer had last stayed with her about five years ago and she lived in a beautiful cottage right by the beach. Well, it was beautiful on the outside. She recalled it was incredibly dated on the inside – not that this bothered Summer. She was rather a fan of the 1970s kitchen and decor.

She called Sylvie that day but no answer. She tried again in the evening, and then again the following day. In the end, she tried her mobile number instead. A strange ringtone.

'Sylvie! It's Summer.'

'Darling, this is crazy! I dreamt about you last night. A premonition, perhaps . . . How are you? And Seth and those handsome boys?'

'All well, but look – I have something to ask you. I don't suppose I could come and stay for a bit, could I?' Summer summarised the details, trying not to make Seth sound like a villain, though this was actually quite difficult.

'What a fool that man is. I've always liked him but I knew the day I met him there was something about his energy . . . It doesn't surprise me he'd do something like this. But I'm sorry, darling, I'm away from Jersey at the moment. I'm in India. You know it's my second home these days. But listen, you can have Mandla. For as long as you like. I rent it out to holidaymakers in the summer but I'll cancel them.'

'Oh no, Sylvie, you can't do that. I'll never be able to match the income you'd get.'

'Nonsense. Family's more important. Anyway, you know me – thanks to my serial husbands, money is something I very fortunately don't need to trouble myself about.'

'But what about the poor people who've booked it?'

'Not a problem. There are some new holiday lets round the corner – my pal Dennis owns them. He told me before I left for India that they're ready earlier than expected so he hasn't set about renting them out this summer. He'll be glad of the income. Now, Mrs Le Feuvre is in charge of the cottage. Let me give you her number.' Summer scribbled it down. 'Phyllis, she's called, but don't ring her after eight in the evening. She hits the whisky bottle and makes no sense at all. I'll give her a quick tinkle so she knows what's happening. Look, must dash – my beau has just turned up. Enjoy Mandla – take it for six months, longer, whatever. Much love!'

She was gone, leaving Summer to marvel at her generosity. Six months in a cottage by the sea in Jersey. Suddenly, the marital break was looking a lot more alluring.

Chapter Five

Jersey, Saturday

Jude

The weekend. He'd made it and felt as triumphant as a climber reaching the peak of Mount Everest to have waded through five days of client complaints and office politics, arriving tired, wrung out and relieved at the best morning of the week – Saturday. Jude stretched out luxuriously and checked his watch. It was absurdly early – his body clock always seemed to adjust to the early starts on the very day he could lie in. But at least he didn't have to get up. He pulled the duvet round him and was just dozing off again when it began. The weekly ritual of the neighbours above, who, for some peculiar reason, reached the height of their lust for each other on a Saturday morning, serving to highlight, depressingly, Jude's own sorry lack of love life. He tried putting a pillow over his head but it was no good. He got up and walked to the kitchen, where he put the radio on and made coffee. He sat on a stool at the counter and blew on his drink. The wall clock told him it was five past seven and he suddenly found himself thinking of the weekend ahead not with his previous muted sense of anticipation but with a slight feeling of panic at the emptiness that lay before him.

He began pathetically scrolling through the contacts on his phone. Two of his best mates – Lee and Ben – were away this weekend and they were his only fellow singletons, James having recently married Donna, who, while unarguably beautiful, was also unarguably demanding. Eddie, meanwhile, was the first of the gang to have had children with his plucky Portuguese girlfriend, Catarina, and would no doubt jump at the chance of meeting up with Jude, but there was always a risk he'd bring the kids with him and Jude would have to suffer the torture of a pub with a soft-play area. His last experience at a child-friendly pub was not one he was in a hurry to repeat.

'Keep an eye on the kids for me a minute, will you?' Eddie had asked. 'Just need the bog.'

'Sure,' Jude had replied, sipping his beer and observing the caged pit opposite in which small children were careering about, hollering. He'd opened his newspaper but hadn't been able to concentrate on it with all the din going on.

'Where's Daddy?'

Jude looked up. Eddie's elder offspring – a girl aged about six, with pigtails – had turned up beside him, looking panicked.

'It's okay – he's just in the loo.'

'You've got to help. Jorge's stuck. Quick!' she said, grabbing hold of Jude's hand. He looked around helplessly but there was no sign of Eddie.

'You've got to take your shoes off!' Rosana said as they entered the play area. She looked at Jude incredulously. Her face told him quite clearly that she thought he was very, very stupid indeed.

Shell-toes disposed of, Jude followed her in, where he found Jorge, who was a little on the portly side, stuck in some hole the kids were meant to wriggle through. Poor boy – he looked just like Winnie the Pooh. His chubby little face poked out one end and he looked at Jude imploringly. Jude rolled up his sleeves and pulled until – all at once – Jorge came flying out of the hole, landing on top of Jude and promptly throwing up all over him.

Eddie looked appalled when he eventually returned from the loo to find Jude covered in vomit and both his children crying.

'What happened?' he asked. Jude told him and, having calmed the kids down (remarkably, they ran back into the dreaded play area again – the bit that hadn't been cordoned off for cleaning), Eddie couldn't stop laughing.

'I'm sorry!' he said. 'You get used to this kind of crap when you're a parent. Do you want a baby wipe?' he asked, hunting around in his backpack.

'Not sure that'll cut it,' Jude replied and, after draining his beer, he returned home for a shower and sank gratefully into his sofa to recuperate in peace.

No, he was better off spending the weekend in solitary confinement. Perhaps he'd give Daisy a call – his mum thought she'd gone 'off grid'. He should check she was okay. First, though, he would nip to the market for a cooked breakfast at his favourite café.

Though still early, the central market was in full swing, the bright-red gates all open, and it smelt like Saturday mornings should – of fresh foliage from the various flower stalls, newly baked bread from the bakeries, and strong, brewing coffee. There were a number of cafés in the market but he was a creature of habit and never deviated from Bisson's, despite the fact that the owner, Mrs Bisson, was a sour-faced woman who seemed to find the fact that Jude wished to order worthy of a deep sigh on every occasion. Still, the breakfast was good – decent coffee and a plateful of sausages, bacon, eggs over-easy (though he was not to use that expression within earshot of Mrs Bisson, who was not keen on Americanisms) and a grilled tomato or two, which Jude considered ample in terms of vitamins. Mrs Bisson always served two rounds of toast after the fry-up 'to round off', which Jude smeared with her home-made marmalade. Delicious, though Jude had learnt not to bother complimenting her on this or anything else. For some reason, Mrs Bisson received praise like most people handle insults.

By the time Jude finished, it was ten and definitely an acceptable time to call his sister. He wouldn't ring her from the café – Mrs Bisson had made it clear she thought mobile phones the work of the devil – but would meander through the cobbled streets and make his way to the waterfront, where he could ogle the yachts while he chatted to Daisy.

'Dais, it's me, Jude.' He sat down on a bench and inhaled the ozone scent of the seawater.

'Oh, hi, Jude,' she said, yawning. 'Hang on a sec.' He heard her muttering to someone. A few steps, then she asked, 'So what's up?'

'Mum says you've gone off grid,' he said, irony in his voice. A seagull flew overhead, squawking loudly.

'Only to her. I've got a new lover and she'll suss me out in no time. She'll want to know all about it. And, well, let's just say this one's different . . .' She clammed up and Jude didn't push her. Daisy had a rampant love life but – like Jude – had never been serious about anyone before.

'How's work?' Jude asked.

'*Mind-blowingly* manic,' Daisy said, but he could hear she was smiling. She adored her job as an A&E doctor – she thrived on the drama and adrenaline and it was this drive of Daisy's that set the siblings apart even more than their looks. (Daisy was as petite and red-headed as Jude was tall and blonde.) She seemed to have enough ambition for the both of them. 'How about you? How's work, life . . . everything?'

'Still crap. I'm feeling lost, Dais. This despondency is starting to affect me physically – I'm getting headaches, feeling really tired . . .'

'You need to get away,' Daisy told him. 'I'm always telling you – Jersey's too small. You'll never meet anyone in that teeny-tiny fish pond. Look, come and stay with me. I can introduce you to Sam at the same time. And don't say yes and then put it off for ever. Promise me you'll look at flights today,' she bossed.

'Okay,' Jude said, without a huge amount of enthusiasm. He loved Daisy but staying with her was exhausting – a relentless timetable of museums, art galleries and social gatherings among her enormous group of friends in trendy bars and expensive restaurants. Plus, he hated London. That great seething mass of humanity and pollution. The only good thing about it was that he was always extraordinarily happy to return home after a few days in the Big Smoke. For that, it was probably worth it. And he had to admit it would be something different to do. 'Promise,' he added. 'I'll book it for next weekend.'

'Perfect,' said Daisy. 'My birthday!'

Jude headed back towards his flat. It was now nearly eleven and town was heaving with Saturday shoppers and French exchange students. He tried not to feel impatient as he was held up by people trudging along talking on their phones (why did talking on a phone make everyone so *slow*?) and, as he dithered about which shop might sell him a birthday present for Daisy, he braced himself for bumping into various people he knew.

The unofficial law of Jersey was that if you were feeling happy and cheery and looking your best, you could walk through town and not come across a single familiar face; but should you be feeling a little glum and introspective or suffering with an unwelcome bout of teenage-style zits, you'd almost certainly bump into at least half a dozen acquaintances.

He turned left into one of the department stores, opting for the cosmetics counter, and stared warily at one of the white-coated women.

'After some make-up?' said a husky voice, with a hint of laughter. Jude looked around in relief – his friend Eddie's girlfriend, Catarina, amusement glinting in her dark eyes. It could be a lot worse.

'Cat! Just trying to choose a birthday present for Daisy.'

'That brand's shite. Clarins would be better. Or, if your budget can stretch, I know just the thing. Follow me.'

Jude did as he was told and followed Cat past various counters where formidable-looking orange-coloured ladies eyed him beadily. Eventually they came upon a counter where a woman looked up from arranging products. Her expression was disdainful.

'Yes?' she asked.

'Madam, I have a potential customer for you, so break a smile,' Cat told the woman, not pulling any punches. Cat really didn't care what anyone thought of her and Jude loved that about her.

The woman looked shocked, then tried her best to smile. 'Are you interested in ze cream or ze serum or ze eye serum or ze lip balm?' she asked in a French accent. Jude looked at Cat rather desperately.

'The classic cream. It's called Crème de la Mer,' Cat told Jude, pushing back her thick, dark hair. 'Every woman's heard of it and not many of us are lucky enough to have tried the stuff. Meant to be the dog's bollocks. How much is it?' she asked the saleswoman, who was having trouble not blanching at Cat's crudity.

'It is one 'undred and forty pounds, sir,' she said, clearly deciding to deal directly with Jude.

'Crap's sake,' said Cat. 'Forget it!' she laughed, but Jude had his card out, ready to pay. 'You're not getting it, are you?' she asked incredulously.

'I usually spend about that on Daisy, so it's okay. If the cream's good . . .' Jude handed over his card and the saleswoman fussed about, decorating the box with a bow and finding a smart-looking carrier bag.

'Bloody hell,' said Cat. 'I wish you were my brother. Lucky if I get a shitty box of chocolates from Cristiano. Right, well, I'd better get on. Glad I could help, anyway.'

Jude smiled at her. 'You did. Thanks, Cat. See you soon!'

She waved and disappeared, a tall figure striding across the shop floor. Jude took his card and the bag containing the expensive pot of magic cream.

'*Au revoir!*' the saleswoman called out.

Jude emerged thankfully into the fresh air, though his nostrils still felt contaminated by the sickly scent of perfumes, then walked briskly through town to his flat. He immediately found his laptop and booked his flight.

Arrive 11.30 on your birthday, leave on Sunday, he texted Daisy. Can't wait to see you!

Enthusiasm. Not Jude's strongest point. But he realised that, actually, he felt a little brighter. A day or two off the Rock. Perhaps that was just the medicine he needed.

Chapter Six

England, Saturday

Summer

Summer pulled out her suitcase and tried to decide what to pack. It was just over a week until she was due to leave but she was trying to be organised about her departure rather than leaving the packing until the last minute as she would usually. She cast a desultory glance into her wardrobe but, uninspired, turned to the bookshelf by the bed instead, with a view to deciding which paperbacks to take with her.

She noticed she'd stuffed several photo albums on the shelf, so she pulled them out and blew off the dust. The first was filled with baby photos of the twins and she browsed through them, kneeling on the floor, although she quickly flicked over the pictures from when the boys had just been born. Despite rushing through the early pages, she caught sight of her face in one photo and realised that she'd looked like a ghost – haunted. She regretted so much that she hadn't 'glowed' like so many other new mothers.

She sighed and quickly moved on to the period when she'd begun to feel better, experiencing a strong maternal pang as she recognised, not for the first time, that one of the most precious times in her life was over. Had been over for years, in fact. As she looked through the pictures of the boys in matching outfits, achieving their milestones, she glossed over the memories of the sleepless nights, the panic when they were unwell and the never-ending dirty nappies. Instead, she popped on her rose-tinted spectacles and spent several moments recalling the blissful smell of her babies – a scent that surpassed all others – and how she'd cradled them to her chest, sometimes both at the same time. The feeding she remembered tenderly, too, forgetting about the cracked nipples and tender breasts and reliving the moments when she would gently snooze as she fed, feeling the oxytocin flood through her body as the boys gorged themselves happily. She recalled Seth always bringing her a glass of water and kissing her on the lips, creeping away with a look of utter pride on his face.

Enough. Too much nostalgia. But then, lodged behind the slightly newer albums, she spotted an ancient one. She began to flick through it. Goodness, it really was old – pre-Seth. There were a few pictures of her as a girl, always standing between her mum and dad as their only child – the centre of their universe. Or her mum's, at least – Frank had been a lovely father, but his greatest passion had always been drugs. Vita, though, had consistently treated Summer as the most precious gift and, while Summer's childhood had been unconventional, it had also been confidence-inspiring in so many ways. Her upbringing intrigued Tilly, who'd led a conventional life since the day she was born.

'So were they new-age travellers then?' she'd asked Summer once.

'No, proper travellers. Nomads.'

'But where did you live?'

'All over the world, in communes, tents, vans, even a cave once.' She laughed at Tilly's shocked face. 'But in houses, too, sometimes.'

'But what about school?'

'My mum taught me,' Summer said, and Tilly shook her head.

'I just can't imagine it. Was it awful?'

'Nope. I loved it!'

And it was true. Though she recognised there had been some gaps (a lack of stability that had later attracted her to sensible Seth, for example), Summer had adored her childhood. But no one ever believed her – she only ever seemed to receive looks of pity when she talked about it nowadays.

Towards the end of the album there were pictures of Summer as a teenager. In every one, she wore a huge smile and some kind of 60s or 70s outfit. Her hair and make-up were retro, too, and Summer remembered how influenced she'd been by her parents, even in terms of her own wardrobe – Frank and Vita had been completely stuck in their heyday. Summer jumped up and shoved the photo album into her suitcase, together with the one of the twins as babies, then returned to her wardrobe, found a chair and balanced precariously on it to retrieve a cardboard box that had been living on top of the cupboard since they'd moved in. She hauled it on to the bed.

'Here we are!' Summer said to herself as she opened it up. Inside was a pile of clothes – all things she'd worn when she was about seventeen, before she'd met Seth and had the twins. There were floppy hats, enormous sunglasses, bell-bottom jeans, shift dresses, smock dresses, bell-sleeved tops and A-line skirts. Even some platform shoes, clogs and a pair of Chelsea boots. She tried to remember where she'd have bought these from in the 90s, when everyone else was wearing boot-cut jeans and tight-fitting V-neck tops. Then she realised – of course, they'd been passed down to her by her mother, who'd always been a hoarder, not easy when you're also a nomad. They were genuine clothes from the 60s and 70s. Summer held up a couple of items.

'I wonder . . .' she said, and she quickly stripped off her M&S T-shirt and her black skinny jeans and pulled on a pair of pale-blue bell-bottoms and a blue-and-white tie-dye top. Amazingly, they fitted, and Summer was finally grateful for the tedious hours she spent in the gym with Tilly, who was a complete gym-bunny. Summer pulled back her hair so it was half up and backcombed it at the crown slightly, then found her eyeliner and tried a 60s flick.

'What on earth are you doing?' asked Seth, surprising Summer, who jumped back like a scalded cat.

'Packing,' Summer told him, putting a hand up to her hair self-consciously.

'You look just like you did when we first met,' Seth said quietly, taking stock. Summer gazed back at him and for a moment she wondered if he might be having second thoughts about the break. But then he ruined it. 'Thank goodness fashions change. Hideous jeans!' he half-laughed. 'I was just looking for my charger. Ah, there it is.' He grabbed it and she heard him return to the kitchen and plug in his phone. Feeling stung, Summer found a wipe and took off the eyeliner, simultaneously letting down her hair. She took the outfit off, too, but she didn't put it back in the box.

Instead, she shoved the clothes, together with the rest of the contents of the box, into her suitcase and zipped it up. She wouldn't take any of her boring headmaster's wife clothes with her. This lot would need a wash once she got there, but they were fine. They fitted her. More than that, seeing her old clothes, trying them on – it had felt like coming home.

Chapter Seven

Jersey, Monday

Jude

Admittedly, Mondays were always a bad thing. But this one was particularly bad. He'd woken up with a stinking headache and it wasn't even a hangover. He contemplated calling in sick, but his work ethic was slightly too strong to permit him guilt-free duvet days and if he was going to feel guilty, he might just as well take some aspirin and get to the office.

Having logged in, he put on his headset and began dealing with calls. Soon, however, his head felt like it was going to explode. A migraine, perhaps? He'd never had one before, though he'd had quite a few headaches lately. By eleven it was clear he couldn't stay at work.

'I've got a terrible headache,' he told his manager after knocking on her office door. 'Going to have to head home.'

Peggy looked up sceptically from her desk but then, seeing his face, her expression changed to one of concern. 'You don't look right,' she said. 'Will you be okay getting home?'

'Yes, should be,' he answered, though now it was becoming tricky to get his words out. He staggered out of the office and made his way to a nearby chemist.

'Have you got anything for a migraine?' he asked, clutching the counter. The chemist looked at him, then immediately called a doctor from the next-door surgery. Jude was accompanied through to the doctor's office, feeling like a fool. Was he making a great fuss unnecessarily? Despite the agony he was in, that was his main concern. He sat down heavily on a plastic chair.

'Have you been tired? Getting a lot of headaches recently?' the doctor asked. She was round and cosy-looking, not remotely medical in her appearance, but clearly very capable.

'I have been quite tired. I thought I might be depressed. A few headaches. But this . . . I've never had anything like it.' The doctor stood up and dimmed the lights. A relief.

'Look, this could just be a migraine, but if it's the worst headache you've ever had, I'd rather we got it checked out straight away. I'm going to call the hospital.'

She went out of the room, returning a short while later with another lady. 'This is Davina, our practice nurse,' she explained. 'She's going to drive you to the hospital. I know it's not far, but I'm worried about you trying to walk there. I've spoken to Mr Vibert, the consultant on call, who'll review you in A&E and then most likely give you a CT scan of your brain.'

Jude thought this was all a bit extreme but he went along with it. He didn't have the strength to argue.

The next few hours were a blur. He was reviewed by the consultant and given a scan. He was helped into a hospital bed at some point. Given some medication. Eventually, he slept. He woke in darkness, still aware of a searing pain in his skull, then slept again. By the following morning his head felt better. Still bad, but better. A nurse entered the room.

'I'm so sorry about all this,' Jude said. 'I'm feeling a lot better now. I'll be off in a minute.'

'You're not going anywhere,' she told him ominously. 'Let me just page Mr Vibert.' But she didn't need to. He was there, in the room, a moment later.

'I'm so sorry,' the consultant told Jude – looking incredibly serious. Jude felt panic wash over him as Mr Vibert got straight to the point. 'This is hard to tell you . . . Jude, it's clear from the CT scan that you have a brain tumour. I'm afraid it looks malignant,' he explained. 'We'll keep you in for a couple more days, make sure we get your symptoms under control. And we'll need to carry out another scan – an MRI this time – to determine what grade the tumour is and its exact position. It's hard to tell from the CT scan whether we'll be able to operate or not. If we *can* operate, I'm afraid the procedure will have to be carried out by a surgeon in Southampton as we simply don't have the expertise here.'

Jude's mind was spinning. 'What do you mean, if you *can* operate? Can't the tumour just be cut out?'

'It's in a difficult location. I won't know for sure until I get the results of the MRI but it may be too dangerous to remove.'

'And if you can't get rid of it?'

Mr Vibert looked directly at Jude. He had nice eyes, a greenish hazel, soft and sympathetic, the skin around them etched with laughter lines. 'Then I'm afraid your situation would be terminal,' he said.

Jude tried to take in the consultant's words. Could this really be happening to him? This was far too dramatic an event for someone whose life was ordinarily so desperately boring. He almost laughed, feeling a rising sense of hysteria within him. He felt like he was watching one of those weekly medical dramas he hated, but which Daisy made him watch whenever he stayed with her. Daisy. The thought of his sister was like a slap round the face and his desire to laugh immediately extinguished itself.

He made an on-the-spot decision not to tell his family. Not just yet. He needed to digest the news himself first. But he needed to tell someone, not least because he needed stuff from home – his toothbrush, pyjamas, iPad, those sorts of things. He decided on Eddie, who wasn't one to make a fuss about anything.

Jude rang and explained everything. Eddie was unusually quiet, then, 'I'm gutted for you, mate,' he kept repeating. Poor Eddie, he clearly didn't know how to handle it – which made two of them. 'Can I do anything?' he asked eventually.

'Please. Can I give you a list of things to get me from home? I'm going to be in for a couple of days. There's a spare key with Mrs De Freitas on the first floor. Let me tell you what I need . . .' He listed the items. 'Could you ring work for me, too? Say I've got a sick bug. Explain I should be back in on Monday.'

'Will do, mate.'

Jude closed his eyes, wishing more than anything that he could wake up from this nightmare and find himself back in his boring job, answering telephone calls and trying to avoid Helena. How could he have taken even a moment of his life for granted before now? He felt as though what was happening to him was like some sort of parable – *look at what happens when you fail to make the most of the gift of life.* It was a bitter pill to try to swallow.

An hour after Jude's MRI scan, as he was waiting anxiously for the results, Cat burst into his hospital room lugging a large rucksack, presumably filled with Jude's belongings.

'Bloody hell, Jude, this is the shittiest thing!' She paused – they'd always been friendly, but never affectionate – then she clearly decided new rules applied and she bounded over to the bed and gave him an enormous hug. Strong and unemotional until that moment, Jude began to cry. Cat just carried on hugging, cushioning his sobs.

'I'm so sorry,' Jude managed eventually. 'It's just . . . you being nice. I've held it together until now.'

'Jude, you really don't need to effing apologise,' Cat told him, her voice husky from too much smoking and talking. She was always swearing – all that time working in a reporters' office for the local news channel – but a crisis really upped the ante. 'What a completely crappy thing to happen. Let me pour you some water, then you can tell me all about it. Here you go. Now budge over.' Cat hopped up on to the bed and listened as Jude told her what he'd learnt so far.

'It definitely looks like a malignant tumour – the consultant can tell from the CT scan. It's awkwardly placed, which is why he isn't sure if the surgeon in Southampton will be able to get rid of it. The question is, what kind of tumour and whether there's any possibility of cutting it out, which should be clear from the MRI. It's a waiting game for now. I'm just so scared, Cat. What if there's nothing they can do?'

'That's the total worst-case scenario – you'll be fine,' Cat reassured him, though Jude thought she looked almost as terrified as he felt. 'Let's try not to worry until we know what we're dealing with.' Then she rummaged around in her handbag, searching for something. Finally, she whipped out a pack of cards. 'Now, come on,' she said, clearly determined to provide a distraction. 'Let's have a game of rummy.'

When Jude received the results of the MRI, Cat was still with him. He supposed Eddie must have been looking after the kids all the while she'd been there. He was unspeakably grateful to have her by his side.

'How'd it go?' Jude asked Mr Vibert.

'I'm afraid it's bad news, Jude,' he said, taking a direct yet kindly approach again. 'The tumour is a grade 4 glioblastoma. One of the most malignant tumours there is. It's on the right side, touching three sides of your brain – the temporal, parietal and occipital lobes. Operating to remove the tumour is not an option. It's far too risky.'

'But don't you need to do one of those operations to check whether it's malignant or not?'

'A biopsy? We certainly can, if you'd like. It's not absolutely necessary, as the scanner we have is very accurate, but it's up to you. You'd need to have the operation in Southampton. Shall I make arrangements?'

Jude paused, then shook his head. 'No. No, I don't see the point in going through all that just to confirm what's clear from the scan. How about chemo? Radiotherapy?'

'I'm afraid there is no cure. At best, chemo would prolong your life slightly – but at some cost. It'll make you feel grotty. Jude, to be totally honest, if I were you I'd just concentrate on enjoying the time you have left.'

Cat squeezed Jude's hand. He looked at her and saw her face was wet with tears. His mouth felt dry and he longed suddenly for a nice hot drink. Images flashed through his mind, as if he were about to die imminently. His parents – how could he be expected to tell them this news? His sister. The lovely house in St Brelade he'd grown up in. The school he'd taught at, which he'd loved so much until the horrendous stabbing episode. His grandmother, who'd lived through the Nazi occupation of Jersey and whose history he suddenly realised he knew so little about . . . He saw that Mr Vibert was watching him anxiously. 'How . . . how long have I got?' he asked, dreading the answer.

'A year, at best. I'm so very sorry. I know it's a lot to take in, but do you have any other questions?'

'Yes,' said Jude, licking his lips. He had a million questions but he decided to start with the easiest. 'Could I have a cup of tea?'

Chapter Eight

England, Monday

Summer

'When do you leave?' asked Tilly as she whipped cream in the Perspex bowl in front of her.

'On Sunday. My final penance is to host dinner on Friday night for Paula,' Summer said, grimacing at the thought of her mother-in-law. 'But I just keep imagining how amazing it'll be to have six months without her to worry about. It's so ironic that someone who comes up with as many clichés as Seth does should have delivered the ultimate one – the battleaxe mother-in-law.'

'I still can't believe you're leaving so soon.'

'It seems to have come round so quickly. What shall I cook on Friday, do you think?'

'Leave it to me,' said Tilly. 'Think of it as my parting gift.' Summer smiled. More than anything, she realised, she'd miss her friend.

◆　◆　◆

On Friday evening, Tilly came up trumps with the meal, but even a gourmet three-course feast wasn't enough to placate Paula. Fortunately, however, it was Seth who was in her bad books – being the instigator of the marital break.

'This wouldn't have happened in my day,' Paula told him sternly as she sipped her soup. She dabbed at her mouth delicately with a napkin. Summer was always amused by how genteel she tried to come across. She'd witnessed her mother-in-law's true colours during several rows between Paula and Seth, when she'd sworn at him like a trooper and even thrown crockery (clearly a family trait, as Seth wasn't averse to the odd plate-throwing episode either). 'Once you've made your bed, you jolly well lie in it,' she continued.

Seth just gave her a dark look, leaving Summer to field her stream of acerbic observations.

'It's just a break,' Summer tried to explain. Having had such a good relationship with her own mother, she'd always pitied Seth the one he had with Paula, and she found herself sticking up for him now out of habit, even though a part of her still felt rejected.

'A break from what? A marriage isn't some kind of office job that comes with twenty days' holiday a year. In which part of your vows did you promise each other a marital break, should you start to feel a bit bored with one another? Your father and I were sick of each other by the time we were forty, but we carried on. That's what you do.'

Summer had to stifle a bubble of laughter at her archaic attitude. She realised that, though the evening was turning out to be an endurance test, it was actually quite helpful. She found herself feeling progressively more supportive of Seth's 'break' idea as the evening went on.

By pudding, Summer's neck was tense and Seth had begun to grind his teeth. She'd never been so pleased to deal with all the clearing up, leaving Seth and Paula to glower at each other. She started stacking the dishwasher as slowly as possible, then, with that job done, she flicked the kettle on and made coffee. Eventually she rejoined the others and was relieved to see they'd called some sort of truce and were on to more benign topics of conversation. As soon as Summer appeared, though, Paula turned her attention to her daughter-in-law – this time with the more pleasant, breezy tone Summer recognised as the one she adopted when she was about to start prying.

'And what are you going to do, then, dear, while you're in Jersey?'

'Same job, different place. One of the benefits of journalism.'

'Ah yes, your little job. Maud from the WI used to live in Jersey. Says it's frightfully expensive. Will you manage okay – you know, with rent and so on?'

'My aunt's lending me her cottage – she's not charging.'

'Oooh, fancy! Always thought it strange how la-di-da your mother and her sister are, considering they're supposed to be hippies. Is it all an affectation, the hippy nonsense, I wonder . . . ?' Then, realising she'd become sidetracked, she asked, 'Is it somewhere nice – the cottage?'

'By the beach, actually,' Summer replied.

'Sounds like a holiday to me. Well, I hope you won't be terribly lonely. Or, for that matter, too un-lonely,' she tittered.

Enough was enough. 'Actually, I've got a bit of a headache coming on. I'm so sorry, but I think I'm going to have to head to bed. Paula, thanks so much for coming round. Look after Seth for me,' she said, kissing her on each cheek. She smelt of out-of-date face powder and lavender talc.

'I'll do my best,' sighed Paula. 'Though a mother is no substitute for a wife.'

Certainly not one as vile as you, Summer thought to herself as she made her exit. She stubbed her toe on her suitcase as she climbed into bed, but it didn't make her yelp. Instead, it made her smile. It was a reminder that an escape was just around the corner.

Chapter Nine

Jersey, Thursday

Jude

On Thursday, Jude was still in hospital, but he felt much better – physically, at least.

A brusque nurse with grey curls had told him earlier that day that he was bound to suffer a lot of symptoms from now on – not just the headaches and lethargy he'd encountered so far. Most of the staff he'd come across had been lovely, but this particular nurse was clearly in the wrong job. She'd run through his potential symptoms in a tone that could only be described as enthusiastic. She might just as well have cackled in a villainous manner when she reached the end of the list.

'Visual disturbances, nausea, dizzy spells, your movement may be affected . . .' she'd forewarned, with an exaggerated frown.

Jude had interrupted. 'Thank you,' he'd said dryly. 'You've been incredibly reassuring.'

'Just warning you!' she'd replied, immediately riled and defensive. 'You wouldn't thank me if you thought it was going to be an easy ride and then you're struck down out of the blue!'

Jude had decided not to explain that he'd have slightly preferred to remain in the dark about her doom-mongering list.

And anyway, for now, at least, he felt fine. He was a bit impatient, to be honest, which was odd considering his whole world had just turned upside down. It had all started as a result of a conversation with an old man he'd come across in the corridor the evening before. The chap, wearing stripy pyjamas and with wispy white hair that looked like it was trying to grow back after chemo, had taken one look at Jude and stopped him with a gnarled old hand.

'You've had bad news,' he said. His hand felt dry and comforting. 'I can see it written all over your face.'

Jude had been slightly taken aback. 'Yes,' he agreed. 'I've got a brain tumour. It's terminal.' He could barely believe those words were coming out of his mouth.

The man had shaken his head. 'You're too young to die. You've barely lived. Mind you, I've got to the ripe old age of eighty and I've not left any sort of positive mark on the world. I was a terrible husband, a useless father, a mediocre employee . . . I haven't been a *bad* man but I haven't been *good* either. When I die, which will be soon, no one will miss me or remember me as someone who achieved anything . . . as someone who cast any sort of light on the world. You take my advice,' he said, gripping Jude's hand harder. 'If you've got any time left, then use it well. Don't die alone, like I will.'

Jude had returned to his room feeling desperately sad but, since that chat, he'd felt a little like he'd had some kind of energising shot in the arm. He wanted to get out of hospital, to start living his life. What was left of it. His phone bleeped.

A text from Daisy: Can't wait to see you tomorrow! Your room is all ready! Xoxoxo

Jude had forgotten about his trip to London. Did he need to cancel it? But then, why couldn't he go? In fact, it was perfect timing. He could explain everything to Daisy face-to-face, rather than over the phone. And what harm could it do? He was dying anyway, after all.

'Am I okay to travel?' Jude asked his consultant later the same day.

'When were you thinking?' Mr Vibert looked hesitant.

'Tomorrow? Just to London. I know I haven't even been discharged yet, but I really want to see my sister. I haven't told her . . .' He looked at the man beseechingly. 'She's a doctor!' he added, suddenly inspired. 'She'll be able to look after me.'

'Hmmm. Well, ordinarily I'd be telling you to take it extremely easy – just pottering about at home, no work for a few more days, no gadding about. I'll tell you what. I'll discharge you today, but please give your sister my number and let her know that I'm happy to discuss your care with her if she wishes,' Mr Vibert said, jotting down his number on a slip of paper and handing it to Jude. 'You'll just need to sign a patient confidentiality waiver so I can discuss everything with her. And no running about! Just gentle plodding . . . Promise?'

'Promise,' Jude agreed.

He arrived at Daisy's flat in Notting Hill just in time for lunch and found his sister fussing about, laying the table for three. She looked nervous.

He started to sing a Stevie Wonder number, a tradition he and his sister had embraced from a young age whenever it was either of their birthdays. 'Ha-ppy biiirthday to ya! Ha-ppy biiirthday to ya! Ha-ppy birthdayyy!'

'Oh Jude! It's so fab to see you!' she said, giving him a big hug. 'I've got so much planned for us. There's this new restaurant opening in town and masses of friends are going to meet us there, including this gorgeous girl called Giselle you haven't met before . . .'

Jude felt panic setting in as she listed all her plans. 'Wait,' he said, stopping her mid-flow. 'Dais, there's something I need to tell you . . . I'd better explain,' he said, and he began.

When he got to the bit about the tumour being inoperable, Daisy interrupted and began to gabble, not letting Jude finish – as if she couldn't bear to hear the end of the story. 'Is chemo an option? Or radiation?' she said, her mouth smiling though her eyes looked wild. 'You'll be fine, Jude, I'm sure of it!'

Jude shook his head. 'No . . . Daisy, it's terminal.'

Daisy burst into tears, her whole body shaking. 'But this is the *very worst* thing I've *ever* heard,' she sobbed. 'Have you told Mum and Dad?'

'No, and I'm not going to just yet. I need time to digest it all. Promise you won't tell them?'

'Okay,' she agreed, sniffing and shuddering. Jude handed her some tissues and they hugged again. At that moment, an attractive woman with peroxide-blonde hair and lots of piercings entered the kitchen.

'Oh, sorry!' she said. 'Have I interrupted something? Are you okay, Daisy?'

'This is Sam,' Daisy explained to Jude, desperately wiping away her tears. 'You know, *Sam*.' Jude didn't understand the emphasis. Who the hell was Sam? He looked confused.

'Huh! My lover, you utter dope! My girlfriend, partner, whatever . . .' Daisy blushed.

'Oh, I see!' Jude exclaimed, the penny finally dropping. So *this* explained why his sister hadn't had any luck in love before now. She'd been barking up the wrong tree. 'Pleased to meet you,' he said to Sam, and they shook hands. Sam had a soft Canadian accent and – despite her outwardly confident appearance – seemed sweet and shy.

Daisy pulled herself together and, after she'd called Jude's consultant, they all had lunch, at which explanations were made about the two great revelations of the day. A bottle of wine broke the ice between Jude and Sam, and Daisy was clearly extremely happy about this, though intermittently Jude caught her staring at him sadly, her eyes frequently threatening tears.

By the early evening, though, Daisy's default positive approach had come to the fore. 'Right,' she said as she sat next to him on the sofa. 'I've been on the phone to a friend who's a trainee neuro-oncologist and he's given me the contact details of an amazing neurosurgeon in London, so I suggest we start by getting a second opinion. Then I've got another pal who's a nutritionist and I've spoken to her and she's going to create a health plan for you so you can take an alternative approach as well. Her boyfriend's an acupuncturist and works *wonders*, so we'll get you booked in with him . . .'

'Dais, stop,' Jude said gently. 'You don't understand. I don't want to fight this. I don't want to waste time chasing second opinions and drinking disgusting juices in the months I've got left. I want to embrace life. It's crazy, but the diagnosis has been like a massive kick up the bum. I just want to enjoy myself.'

Daisy sank back on the sofa, deflated. 'I don't understand . . . If it was me, I just couldn't accept it.'

'Look, it's not that I've accepted it as such. In fact, I don't want to think about it all. I just don't want to waste precious time doing stuff I feel is futile. I'm too cynical for all that. It might work for someone like you, because you'd *believe* it. But for a jaded old git like me, it's just not going to.'

Daisy sighed. 'I see your point . . . But Jude, how do you intend to enjoy the time you've got left? You don't exactly lead a *riveting* life in Jersey. Do you want to move in with us?' she asked, excited at the thought.

'I'll come and stay more, but no – kind though your offer is, I'm going to head back home after this weekend. I'll hand my notice in at work, see if I can find a new place to rent by the sea. I might even join an online dating agency, like you've suggested before. I may be dying, Dais, but I'll tell you now – I'm finally going to start living.'

Daisy looked like she was going to start crying again but with superhuman effort she smiled instead. 'Let's start tonight, then. Let's go somewhere *tremendous* for dinner. Not the restaurant opening – my friends won't mind. A quiet place where it's just us. But somewhere memorable. Jude, I do love you.'

'Me too,' Jude said, squeezing his sister to him. He thought about the wise words from the old man in the hospital and knew that at least he could count on Daisy and the rest of his family and friends. He wouldn't die alone.

Chapter Ten

Jersey, Sunday

Summer

It might have been a fluke but, arriving in Jersey in May and stepping off the plane, Summer felt like she'd landed somewhere tropical, not a British island just half an hour from London. A balmy breeze enveloped her as she descended the plane steps, the sort of warmth that felt like a caress.

The journey by taxi from the airport to Mandla was very stop-start – not because there was a lot of traffic, but because the drivers were endlessly polite to one another, going to great lengths to let each other out. As they turned right at Waitrose in St Brelade, Summer noticed a series of cars flashing their lights at the taxi driver.

'Why are they flashing?' she asked.

'There'll be a police officer along this road with a speedometer. They're warning me,' the man replied, lifting a hand to thank the drivers in the opposite direction. He slowed down. A place of courteous drivers. It had been years since she'd been to Jersey and she'd forgotten its charming idiosyncrasies. She remembered now. What else did she recall from her last trip? The sea – nearly always visible and so clean and clear and inviting. Long, sandy beaches on the west of the island, craggy cliffs in the north and the beautiful, tranquil harbours of Gorey and St Aubin. Red squirrels scuttling up trees. £1 notes. Ducks crossing the road with their ducklings following at a leisurely pace. Farmers plodding along the lanes with their herds of dairy cows – no rush, cars just waiting patiently. The Franglaise feel to the place – so utterly Cornish in many ways, yet with French road names, delicious baguettes and a certain *je ne sais quoi* to the atmosphere that made it just *seem* French.

'That's it, the next right after those apartments,' Summer told the taxi driver as the car swept down the hill. 'Perfect. If you could just pull up on the left . . .' The cottage was small but looked instantly welcoming and coastal, with lobster pots stacked up along one side of the exterior. It had been newly painted a crisp white and a string of bright pink buoys had been hung like balloons along the outside wall. Mandla looked striking.

'Beautiful spot,' the driver remarked.

'Isn't it?' Summer agreed. She'd forgotten just how close to the tiny cove at Petit Port the cottage was. It was perched just above the beach with the most incredible view of the ocean, Corbière lighthouse in the distance. On a beautiful early-summer's day like this, it was breath-taking.

Summer paid for the journey then wheeled her case along the path to the back door, where, as promised by Mrs Le Feuvre, the key was hidden under the doormat.

She opened the door, expecting to enter the pure 1970s lime-green kitchen she remembered from her last visit, and gasped out loud to find herself standing in the most pristine, welcoming and tasteful kitchen she'd ever had the pleasure to encounter.

It was an oblong room – not huge, but perfectly proportioned – with white New-England-style cupboards, a butler sink with jewel-coloured splash-back tiles above it, oak working surfaces and sand-coloured flagstones. Within a recess on the right-hand wall was a dark-blue Aga and beside it was an armchair dressed with two plump cushions. On the other side of the room there was a round oak table with four matching chairs and in the centre of the table was a ceramic jug filled with Jersey lilies. The room felt warm, cosy. Settled.

'Wow!' Summer said to herself. She abandoned her case in the kitchen and went to explore the rest of the cottage. She discovered the entire place had been revamped. A door led from the kitchen straight through to the south-facing living area – a long room with enormous windows providing the perfect combination of wall-to-wall sea views bathed in day-long sunshine.

Patio doors led on to a terrace but Summer stayed inside for now, taking in all the beautiful details of the living room. Two generous sofas and an armchair, all upholstered in soft grey linen and scattered with pink cushions. Walls washed white with the merest hint of pink and grey tones. The central feature of the room (aside from the view) was a cream wood-burning stove. Above the fireplace was an exquisite coastal painting and in front was a glass coffee table on which was stacked a neat pile of glossy magazines. The numerous lamps dotted around the room were nautically themed – huge cream lampshades balancing on models of lighthouses, boats and beach huts. It was like something out of an interiors magazine. Summer knew her aunt had received a decent divorce settlement from her latest ex-husband but she hadn't realised until now quite how decent it must have been. Sylvie had gone to town on the place.

There was also a bathroom and a twin room, then – next to that – a door opened to a bedroom that shared the sea views of the living area. The windows were open and a breeze made the soft pink curtains quiver. A breeze that smelt of salt and sand and sunshine. Opposite the windows was an enormous bed covered with starched white linen and scattered with dozens of comfortable-looking pillows and cushions, as well as a grey cashmere blanket. Summer jumped on to the bed and lay back – it was like lying on a cloud. Deliciously comfortable. She wondered how she was going to feel sleeping alone after putting up with Seth's teeth-grinding for so many years. She'd worried she might feel lonely and a little sorry for herself, but there was something about the feel of the cottage that made her realise she was more than likely to enjoy her solitude. And, she realised, for the first time in a very long period she wouldn't have to *pretend*. Her life as a headmaster's wife had been one long pretence – following convention after her laid-back, nomadic childhood – and although she'd been quite happy to make the sacrifice (and had, to some degree, embraced the security her new life offered her), she felt relief at having cast off the shackles of living in a school, married to a difficult man, and conforming in every area of her life.

From the comfort of the bed she observed the rest of the room. White plantation shutters on the windows, as well as the long pink curtains. Two white bedside tables, each housing a nautical lamp, magazines and a pitcher of water with a tumbler. The blinds were open so Summer looked out at the scene beyond and could barely believe her luck – the gently undulating sea of an incoming tide, the lighthouse in the distance.

Though she had hardly admitted it at the time, even to herself, she'd been hurt by Seth's decision to have a marital break. Of course she had. But now – having made it to Jersey – she was simply grateful. For being granted an escape from that conventional life. An escape to what had to be the most perfect retreat on earth. She shook off her shoes, snuggled down and decided to enjoy an indulgent afternoon nap.

This was heaven.

PART TWO

Falling in Love

May–mid-August 2017

Chapter Eleven

Jersey, Monday

Jude

He was dying, but he'd never felt so alive. The words of that old man at the hospital still ringing in his ears, Jude had decided to make the most of every second of the life he had left. He'd started by making a bucket list. Not the sort most people would make, but a humble one that reflected the kind of simplicity Jude had been brought up to value. The first item on the list was the most important: '1. Don't die alone.' He was pretty sure he wouldn't – after all, he had his sister, his parents and his friends to count on. But there was also a part of him that wondered if he might just be lucky enough to meet someone – romantically – who would be there with him until the end. The old Jude would have thought that ridiculous – who would be willing to open their heart to someone who was going to die? But the new Jude was more optimistic and he planned to join a dating website as soon as possible.

He'd arrived home from London the night before and, keen to make the most of feeling so unusually full of verve, he ignored the suitcase he ought to unpack and decided to head straight to the office to extricate himself at last from his ball-and-chain job. Fortunately, he'd

Rebecca Boxall

been saving for years for a deposit so he could buy a flat rather than rent for ever, so he had plenty to live on during the time he had left.

Peggy's office door was open but he knocked on it, feeling nervous. 'Come in,' she said, looking up from her desk. 'Oh Jude, are you better? A sick bug, wasn't it?' She looked concerned, though Jude knew that Peggy was extremely averse to catching anything and he could see her trying to calculate whether he was past the contagious stage. He shut the door gently behind him.

'Actually, I'm afraid that wasn't the full truth. I ended up in hospital with that bad headache I had last week. I had some scans carried out and the long and the short of it is that . . . is that I'm dying,' Jude said, tripping over his words.

Peggy looked at him sharply. 'Are you joking?' she asked.

Jude laughed. 'No, Peggy, I'm really dying. I've been given less than a year to live.'

Peggy paled. She put a hand to her mouth. 'Jude, this can't be true . . .'

'It is,' Jude persevered. He wondered if he was going to come up against this sort of resistance with every single person he told the bad news to. The thought was exhausting.

'But . . . but that's dreadful . . . I . . . I don't know what to say.' She looked appalled.

'Look, you don't need to say anything. In fact, please don't. Don't tell anyone else. I'm trying not to think about it all.'

'But what is it?' Peggy asked. 'Is it cancer?' she whispered, hardly daring to say the 'c' word out loud.

'A brain tumour. It's terminal . . .' It was still shocking to say those words. He still felt like this drama should be happening to someone else. 'But, look, I want to finish here and I don't want to have to work the notice period specified under my contract. Time is precious,' he said, smiling ruefully. 'Would that be okay?'

64

'Of course, of course. Finish at the end of this week.' Peggy shuffled some papers on her desk, looking uncomfortable. 'I'll just need a note.'

'A note?'

'From your doctor. If I waive the requirement under your contract for you to work your notice period, I need evidence of your . . . situation . . .'

Jude thought he might laugh out loud. He'd always known Peggy was a stickler for the rules, but really? No doubt there was a section on this very subject in Peggy's management manual. Page 354: *Always ensure you have firm proof that an employee is dying when they ask to leave without working their notice period, just in case they're pulling a fast one on you.*

'Don't you believe me?' he asked her.

'Of course I believe you . . . It's just the rules.'

'Sure it is,' Jude replied, sighing heavily, amusement replaced with a bittersweet realisation that this was probably the last time he'd ever become exasperated by his boss, whose insistence on rule-abiding was pathological. Despite this, Jude felt a deep-seated loyalty towards her, and he wasn't going to give her a hard time. He thought back to the job interview he'd had with Peggy a few months after the stabbing, when he'd left his teaching post and was desperate for an income. The interview had gone appallingly badly and Jude had just resigned himself to the fact that he wouldn't get the job when Peggy posed one last question.

'Why did you leave your old job?' she'd asked. 'It's just, it seems like a bit of a funny leap – from teaching to banking?'

Jude had wondered about coming up with some innocuous reason, but in the end he'd told the truth. 'I was stabbed by a student,' he'd said. 'I'm recovered physically but it was a lot to take on board mentally. Not that my mental health is an issue,' he'd added quickly. He knew that, even in this day and age, employers could be prejudiced against poor mental health.

Peggy, who'd shown herself to be rather brusque until that point, had looked at him sympathetically. 'Ah,' was all she'd said, but the very next day she'd called him up and offered him the position. However dull the job had turned out to be, he would never forget her kindness.

'I'll get you a note by tomorrow,' he said now. 'I'll leave on Friday.'

'One last thing,' Peggy said, smiling weakly – no doubt with relief that this dreadfully awkward meeting was almost finished. 'I won't tell anyone why you're leaving but we'll need to have bubbles and nibbles for you on your last day. Five thirty in reception. I'll organise it.'

Jude's heart sank, but Peggy clearly thought she was doing him an enormous favour.

'Thank you,' he said feebly, and he began to prepare mentally for the end of the week. The day at work felt long – a waste of time – but by twenty past five he was home and, after tripping over his bag, he decided he should probably get round to unpacking it. He hauled it through to the bedroom. It was a huge case – far too large for a weekend – but it was the only luggage he had. On the way out it had been virtually empty, but Daisy had filled it with heavy medical books on brain tumours, which he'd taken to humour her. He'd also been on a shopping trip with his sister – she'd persuaded him to buy virtually a whole new wardrobe, most of it from Superdry. The stuff would make him look like a proper hipster – skinny jeans, tight-fitting shirts, uber-hip jackets and proper shoes – but perhaps it was time for a change from his boring old T-shirts, trainers and boot-cut jeans combo. Particularly if he was going on a dating mission.

He unzipped the large grey case and laughed. Was this a joke? It was filled with women's clothes. He held up a couple of items. Somebody small and fixated on the 60s and 70s, by the look of things. The clothes smelt a bit fusty. There were a couple of photo albums, one full of dated-looking pictures showing someone wearing the clothes in question. She looked about eighteen. He thought at first the photos were old, then wondered if it was just the filter on them. But then he saw the next album – pictures of babies growing into toddlers – and he couldn't believe the tiny young woman in the other album would have kids.

The doorbell rang and Jude hopped up to answer it. It was Cat. Jude was pleased she now felt she could just drop in – something she wouldn't have done before his diagnosis. He realised that this was one of the silver linings to his recent news and Cat's attitude was just what he needed to help him with his quest to seize life by the horns.

'Cat! How are you? Come in . . .'

'Shit day, but okay. Better than you. How you doing?'

'Feeling weirdly positive about life – or what's left of it. I'm making the most of it. But something odd's happened. Come and see.'

Jude took Cat through to the bedroom, where he'd started to unpack the case.

'I've obviously picked up the wrong bag. Which means someone on Sunday afternoon's flight must have mine!'

'Jude, this is perfect. A story for me. Can you let me run with it? I'll do a feature on the news tomorrow. "Young Jerseyman seeks woman who stole his case!"'

'Well, "stole" is a bit strong. She could say the same about me.'

'Whatever. Can I do it?' Cat looked so eager that Jude didn't want to disappoint her. And anyway, he wanted his stuff back so it was worth a punt, however unlikely a successful outcome was. He'd spent a fortune on all his new clothes.

'Go on then,' he agreed, and they went through to the kitchen, where they sat at the counter and Cat made notes for the feature while Jude found a couple of beers and some crisps.

By the end of the evening Cat had the story sewn up. 'Right, watch the news tomorrow morning. Hopefully the bag thief will see it and call up. Bloody exciting!'

Jude stood at the door and waved Cat off. He wondered if anything would come of the news item, but either way he'd made Cat's evening and he felt like he really owed her after her support following his diagnosis.

Jude gave the kitchen a cursory tidy-up, took out his lenses and cleaned his teeth. In his newly optimistic mood, he went to bed feeling more convinced that Cat's suggestion might not be such a long shot after all. Perhaps her news story *would* bring him back his suitcase. For some strange reason, he had the feeling that getting his bag back might be another catalyst for him. It was just a feeling – the sense that something positive could well be just around the corner.

Chapter Twelve

JERSEY, MONDAY

SUMMER

The next thing Summer knew, it was seven o'clock in the morning. She'd only meant to have a nap but the bed had been so comfortable. How incredible to have slept right through. She usually woke up fighting for the duvet with Seth at least once during the night.

She got up to use the bathroom then ran back into the bedroom and jumped on to the bed. She bounced up and down for a minute, laughing with joy at waking up in such an amazing place, then snuggled back against the sumptuous cushions. The blinds and curtains were still open and she could see the tide was high; right up to the sea wall beneath the terrace. She could hear it too, the waves pounding at soothingly regular intervals. She took a deep breath and realised she could even smell the ocean – the scent of purity, a briny, intoxicating freshness.

Summer closed her eyes and carried on breathing deeply. Then she opened them. Something was strange, different. Then she realised – she could see! But it was no miracle. She hadn't taken her contact lenses out when she'd had her afternoon nap. Her eyes felt sore now that she thought about it and a glance in the mirror showed they were red and bloodshot. Oh dear. She hoped she wouldn't get an infection. She would need to try to get them out, but first she'd need her glasses, which were in her suitcase. Which was where? Summer padded out of the bedroom and searched around the cottage, eventually finding the case in the kitchen. She was about to open it when she spotted the kettle. Tea first – essential first thing. She opened the fridge and was amazed to see there was not only cow's milk but soya milk – ideal – and that it was fully stocked with essentials, fruit and vegetables. Even a mini bottle of champagne, which Summer earmarked for the evening. She made a mug of tea and took it outside on to the terrace, where she drank it at the wooden table and relished being splashed with sea spray and feeling the breeze ruffling her hair.

I suppose I ought to unpack, she thought to herself after a while. She returned to the kitchen and grabbed the case, wheeling it along to the bedroom, where she unzipped it.

'What the . . . ?' she asked nobody. 'Oh bugger! Don't tell me I've picked up the wrong case? All my stuff! My glasses, my contact lenses . . . I'm going to be blind. Unless . . .' Feeling a bit cheeky, she unzipped a washbag and found inside a packet of daily contact lenses in a prescription that wasn't far off her own. She laughed. Fortunately for the case's owner, she had several packs of lenses in her own bag. That was something, anyway, but it was clear the similarities between Summer and the other person ended there. These were the clothes of a very young man – a proper hipster. Someone very cool. She checked out the heavy books on brain tumours. A trainee doctor, maybe? Unless. She put a hand to her mouth. What if the man had a brain tumour himself? How awful! And now she'd inadvertently stolen his case.

Not too sure what to do next, she did what she always did in times of indecision. She called Tilly.

'Summer! I've been itching to speak to you. How is it? What's the cottage like? Is it as you remembered?'

'Yes and no . . . The location is just as beautiful but the cottage has been updated and it's sublime. You'd love it! But look, something's happened. You know I've got one of those generic grey suitcases? Well, I picked up the wrong one from the carousel at the airport. I've brought someone else's back to Sylvie's with me. And they must have taken mine.'

'Summer, why on earth didn't you put a distinctive coloured ribbon on it or something?'

'I just didn't think!'

'Honestly, you're priceless. Mind you, clearly this other traveller made the same mistake.'

'And now I have to try to find them. What would you do?'

'Well, I suppose the obvious place to start would be to call the airport. I should think the other person's already phoned and left their details. They're bound to be able to put you in contact with each other.'

'Oh Tilly, why didn't I think of that? Of course, that makes perfect sense.'

'I hope you get it sorted. Oh bother, there's someone at the door. I was longing for a good chat, too. There's something I needed to talk to you about. And, of course, I'm dying to know how you're getting on. Will you text me to let me know what happens about the case? And I'll call in the next couple of days . . .'

'Will do. Thanks, Tilly. Lots of love.'

Summer disconnected the call, wondering what Tilly had wanted to mention, but she soon became sidetracked by searching for the number for the airport.

'I wonder if you can help,' she began after calling it up. 'I accidentally took someone else's suitcase on Sunday afternoon. I'm afraid I've only just found out – I didn't unpack immediately. I'm guessing they'll have been in touch? They must have mine, you see,' Summer explained.

'Let me just check,' said the efficient voice at the other end. A pause and a little tinny music for a few moments. 'I'm sorry. No one's called in. But if you give me your details I'll contact you as soon as anyone rings about it.'

Summer gave her details then hung up. She didn't really want to have to stay in the clothes she was wearing indefinitely. *I'll have a bath,* she thought to herself. *Then I'll take a bus into St Helier and buy a few bits and pieces to tide me over. The goon who's got my case is probably as lazy as me about unpacking. He'll soon realise and then he's bound to call the airport.*

Summer pottered through to the bathroom – truly the loveliest she'd ever come across, with cream mosaic tiles, heated rails bearing enormous fluffy white towels, a state-of-the-art rainforest shower and a luxuriously deep spa bath. It was only as she turned on the taps and poured in some bubble bath that she realised it hadn't actually occurred to *her* to phone the airport. It had been Tilly's idea. She could only hope that this chap – hipster doctor, patient, whoever he was – was slightly more sensible than she was.

After the bath, Summer realised she didn't have a hairdryer. She couldn't remember the last time she'd let her hair dry naturally – a smooth hairstyle had been part of her attempt to look the part of headmaster's wife – but she had no choice, and when she caught sight of herself in a shop mirror later in the day she realised it wasn't so bad. Wavy. It kind of suited her. And how much easier. She decided then and there to leave her hairdryer firmly in the case once she'd finally retrieved it.

By the end of the day Summer had at least acquired a few wardrobe essentials and toiletries to tide her over. She called the airport again but no luck. In the end she decided to crack open the champagne. She rooted around in the fridge and found some vegetables and made a simple stir-fry. She ate her meal out on the terrace but the sea breeze was cool so she soon returned inside, where she ensconced herself on the sofa and happily read her latest novel, enjoying the peace. By ten she could feel her eyes getting heavy and she didn't want to fall asleep with her lenses in again so she got ready for bed and dived into it. As she lay back, she thought about the inconvenience of the lost luggage and what a state Seth would have got into about it. An airline had once lost their suitcases on a holiday to Spain and he'd been out of his mind with anxiety. She felt a little bad for thinking it, but she had to admit how much easier it was to deal with such setbacks without Seth and his simmering rage. He wouldn't have been able to sleep until the case had been returned. Summer, on the other hand, turned on to her side and fell almost instantly into a deep and satisfied slumber.

She woke early the next day – Tuesday – and, after using the bathroom, went through to the living room and flicked on the TV. She went and made herself a cup of tea, then returned and perched on the sofa arm as she cradled the mug. She channel-hopped, eventually settling on a local news programme. About time she took notice of what was going on in the world – even just the confines of this small island.

'And finally,' the newswoman said with a grin, 'the story of a missing suitcase! Local man Jude De Carteret accidentally picked up a bag belonging to someone else after a journey from Gatwick to Jersey last Sunday afternoon. He's assuming a fellow traveller must have made the same mistake and taken his case home. Jude is keen to locate the person, who's believed to be a young woman who wears contact lenses and may have a couple of small children. If you know who the mystery lady might be, please do contact us on the number or email coming up just now on the screen . . . Good luck, Jude . . .'

Summer dived for a pen and piece of paper and scribbled down the details for Channel TV.

'Excellent!' she said to herself. Within half an hour she'd tracked the man down, though he clearly wasn't in a hurry about swapping cases, despite his TV appeal.

I'm working all week so is it okay if we meet on Saturday? he asked by text.

Summer hesitated but decided she could manage a little longer. Sure, that's fine. Shall I tell you where to find me?

I'll text you Sat morning. You can tell me then. Glad I tracked you down, his text read.

Me too!!! Summer replied. She sat and pondered for a moment what the young hipster might look like. She decided he'd be sporting a full beard (they all did these days) and would be short, stocky and dark-haired. In any event, all would be revealed soon enough.

Chapter Thirteen

JUDE'S BUCKET LIST:

1. DON'T DIE ALONE.

As it turned out, Jude was quite right to have been nervous about bubbles and nibbles. It was possibly the most squirm-inducing experience of his life. The main issue was the inquisitiveness. Everyone wanted to know why he was leaving so suddenly.

'How'd you get out of this place then?' asked Bradley, one of the client managers, as he delved into the crisps. Having witnessed the guy fail to wash his hands after using the urinals ten minutes before, Jude made a mental note not to bother with the nibbles.

'Just fancied a change,' Jude replied, using the stock response he'd devised. 'Might do a bit of travelling.'

'Travelling, huh? Bet you're after a bit of totty, aren't you? Not many decent fillies in Jersey these days. All the hotties have been snapped up by the time we get to our age! Mind you, Suki's a bit of all right. Thought you might have been in there . . .'

At this point Helena plodded over, interrupting Bradley. Jude had never been so glad to see her.

'Was it constructive dismissal?' she asked eagerly, looking interested in a pained kind of way. 'I know an employment lawyer if you need one. I know what this place is like . . .'

Helena and her conspiracy theories. Jude took another gulp of warm cava. He could feel a headache coming on. He checked his watch. It was only quarter to six. He'd be expected to stay until at least six thirty and there was always the danger of somebody suggesting they 'go on' for drinks at the Dolphin, or even dinner. He wondered about inventing another arrangement but then, realising it was the last time he'd ever see any of these people – a couple of whom he loathed, true, but most he was extremely fond of – he knew he should just suck it up, embrace it. This was the first, it occurred to him, of many last times.

Helena was in the middle of a long complaint about her least favourite client when Peggy tapped on her glass with a pen.

'If I could have a moment, please!' she called, and Jude realised that, horror of all horrors, she was going to give a speech. 'I just wanted to say a few words about Jude before he leaves us. I know we'll all miss him – he's just one of those sorts who's nice to have around. But what you probably don't know is that Jude very nearly wasn't given the job when he came for interview four years ago!' There was a little burst of laughter around the room and Jude felt Bradley nudging him.

'He was hopeless,' Peggy continued, and Jude had to smile at her bluntness. 'He hadn't carried out any research about the company and he was completely unconvincing when I asked him what aspects of banking appealed to him, and he said he was looking forward to "dealing with client complaints with a smile".' More laughter.

'But then I asked him why he wanted to switch jobs from teaching to banking,' she said, her tone suddenly more serious. 'And I hope you don't mind me revealing this, Jude, but he told me about a traumatic incident that had happened at the school where he'd worked. He was stabbed by one of his students.' There was a collective gasp around the room and Jude felt his cheeks burning, his heart – even now – hammering as he was reminded of that awful experience from his past.

'Jude was left physically and mentally scarred by that harrowing event and yet he gave himself very little time before looking for a new job. I saw then how brave he was and what an asset he'd be to the company. I also wanted to give him a chance because someone very special to me was stabbed a decade ago and, unlike Jude, he didn't make a recovery.' There was silence in the room now, everyone clearly shocked by this uncharacteristic revelation.

'Anyway,' Peggy said, looking directly at Jude, 'I'm glad I gave you that chance. You've been perfectly good at the job but, I have to say, I don't think the bank is your natural habitat. I hope, now, you'll live a life that suits you better,' she added, raising her glass. 'To your good health!' Everyone raised their glasses and then put them down so they could applaud Peggy's rather moving speech.

'Oh, one more thing!' Peggy piped up. 'I have a card and present for you here, Jude, from all the staff at the bank. If you'd like to come and receive them . . .'

Jude went up to Peggy to collect the card and gift, thinking back to the time – not very long ago at all – when he'd wished he might be on the receiving end of one of the greetings cards dished out at work. How ironic that he should be receiving one so soon and under such difficult circumstances. It just went to show you should be careful what you wished for.

All eyes on him, he opened up the card, but found the writing blurring as he read the kind comments, his eyes unexpectedly prickling with tears. He blinked them away and then opened his gift – laughing when he saw it was a year's subscription to Netflix. Suddenly Jude found himself surrounded by his colleagues, patting him on the back and wishing him luck. In the end, he found himself very happily following them all across the road to the Dolphin.

◆ ◆ ◆

The following day – Saturday – he woke up with a hangover. He thought of the evening before and smiled to himself ruefully as he remembered Helena drunkenly attempting to kiss him at the end of the night. He'd made his excuses kindly to the poor woman – although he didn't want to die alone, he was also fairly sure he didn't want Helena by his side, bringing him down in his last moments. But he hoped she wasn't waking up feeling too mortified at the memory.

All he felt like doing was lazing around the flat for the morning but he didn't have time to hang about. He'd promised to meet up with the mystery woman who had his suitcase and he needed to check where she was staying.

Hi, he texted. Jude here – lost suitcase man. Are you still okay to swap bags today? Where do you live?

Hi Jude! I'm on an extended holiday, staying in Petit Port. Do you know it?

Of course – near the lighthouse at Corbière.

That's right. I can meet you there if that's easier for you? It's only a short walk.

A landmark – probably for the best. Great. Is eleven okay?

Perfect!! See you then. I'm small with dark hair and a large suitcase, LOL!!

LOL? And two exclamation marks. As he'd thought, she must be a teenager. In her favour, she'd at least refrained from using any emoji.

Jude arrived bang on eleven and found a space in the car park with its view overlooking the lighthouse and the turbulent sea. It was a fine day, but gusty, and the wind was blowing onshore, stirring up the water and creating messy waves. He scanned the area, but aside from an old couple in anoraks there was nobody in sight. He switched on the radio and prepared himself for a long wait, but moments later he spotted a slightly built female with dark wavy hair wheeling his large suitcase across the tarmac. He immediately hopped out of the car and heaved her bag out of his boot.

'Summer?' he asked, approaching her.

'Jude!' she smiled. He found himself frozen to the spot, unable to respond.

Summer wasn't a teenager. She was a woman. Possibly even a little older than him, given the crow's feet around her vivid blue eyes. He'd never realised that wrinkles could be so sexy. She had a tiny, sun-kissed nose, a pixie face that reminded him of Sandra Bullock (Jude's ultimate pin-up), and she was miniature, though he was soon to find out that her laugh was enormous – an irresistibly dirty giggle. She was beautiful.

Jude desperately tried to think of something to say. His mouth felt dry, his heart was hammering, and yet he also felt hopeful that perhaps fate had brought him and Summer together for a reason. Then he noticed it, as she fiddled with a pendant on a long chain around her neck. A wedding ring.

'Here's your case,' he said, stating the obvious.

'And here's yours!' Summer laughed. 'What a fiasco! I hope you don't mind but I used some of your contacts. I couldn't believe we're almost the same prescription!'

'Er . . . Oh, not at all. I'd have done the same but I had another pack at home.'

A pause. 'Well . . .' Summer said, and they stood there, gazing at each other, the wind whipping around their ears. 'So, I guess I'd better head back.'

'I'll give you a lift,' Jude said, hoping not to sound desperate but unable to part with her just yet, even though it was clear he'd never see her again after today. 'I can fit both the cases in the boot. Save you dragging it along the road.'

'Oh, would you? That would be fab, thank you!'

Jude heaved both cases into the car and was about to get into the driver's seat when Summer's words stopped him. 'Have you ever been out there? To the lighthouse?' she asked.

'Never,' he replied.

'That's terrible!' Summer teased. 'You're an islander, right?'

'We're the worst. Tourists always leave the place knowing it better than the locals.'

'Come on, then. We can explore together!'

Jude couldn't believe Summer was prolonging their moment together, but he wasn't going to give her a chance to have second thoughts. He smiled. 'Okay.' He was about to lock the car when he remembered he'd brought a flask of coffee and some biscuits with him, a hasty hangover cure he'd packed at the last minute before leaving his flat. He was aware of Summer watching as he shoved it all into his backpack, then he hauled the bag on to his shoulder and turned to face her, in some strange way feeling more relaxed now that he knew she was married and that clearly nothing was ever going to happen between them.

'Let's go!'

They left the car and took a steep path down towards the rocks below, clocking the various German bunkers left over from the Second World War and the Nazi occupation. Then, on reaching the bottom of the hill, they took the path that ran between the rocks towards the lighthouse. They didn't chat as they walked but, surprisingly, the silence wasn't awkward.

When they finally reached the lighthouse, white and solid, Summer sat down on a bench. She was the first to speak.

'What a view!' she said, pointing at the expanse of sea all around them and the cliffs in the distance blanketed with pink and yellow flowers – great swathes of sea pink and spotted rock-rose.

'Incredible,' Jude agreed, though he was less interested in their surroundings and far more intrigued by the woman sitting beside him.

'You're ill, aren't you?' she said next, getting straight to the point.

Jude was astonished at her astuteness and found himself reminded of the old man at the hospital. 'I . . . Yes, I am. How did you know?'

'The books on brain tumours in your suitcase were a giveaway. I hoped you might just be a doctor or something. But now I've seen your eyes.'

'My eyes?'

'Yes. They're full of sadness.'

'Shit,' Jude said. He bit his lip, feeling a little vulnerable that his eyes seemed to be giving away his secrets. 'You're right, anyway. A brain tumour. Inoperable. I've got a year to live, at most.' He looked down at the ground, unable to continue to meet Summer's gaze. The next moment he felt a hand on his. A soft, tanned hand – tiny, yet enormously reassuring.

'Why don't you get the coffee and biscuits out?' she suggested. 'A bit of comfort in a crisis.' She said it as if his crisis were hers as well. It felt incredibly consoling. He poured a cup for them to share and Summer opened the biscuits and munched several, one after the other.

'Sorry,' she mumbled. 'I'm into healthy eating usually – I don't eat biscuits much. These ones are delicious!' she giggled. Infectious. Such an infectious laugh. Though a moment later the laughter was drowned out by a sudden, loud siren.

'What's that?' Summer asked.

'Probably a re-enactment or something to do with the German bunkers. A Second World War air-raid siren or something . . .' He wasn't really interested. What he wanted to know was why Summer was in Jersey on an extended holiday and whether her husband was waiting for her back in Petit Port.

'You're married,' he said, taking the same direct approach Summer had with him. He wouldn't usually have had the confidence to be quite so forthright, but a whole new side to him seemed to be emerging since his diagnosis.

'On a break,' Summer explained. 'My husband's back in the UK, busy having a midlife crisis, and I've been packed off to Jersey. Actually, that makes me sound reluctant, which I'm not. I'm loving it. I probably shouldn't be, but I am,' she told him, looking impish.

'Your husband must be insane,' he told her. 'If I were married to you, I—' He stopped himself and looked down. What was he *saying*? She'd think he was a lunatic.

Summer looked at him, seeming amused. 'Well,' she laughed, 'I suspect I'm partly at fault, though heaven knows I'm not sure exactly what it is I'm meant to have done. I'm going to get my friend Tilly on the case. See if she can find out what's going on. But for now I'm just going to enjoy it. The break.'

'You sound like me. I've decided to do the same – just enjoy the time I have left.'

Summer looked at him, serious now, her wild hair lashing his face. It smelt of coconut and vanilla and made him feel quite weak with longing. 'You're brave,' she said. 'You're truly brave.' It was the second time in two days that Jude had been called brave. He didn't think he was at all, but he didn't argue. After a moment, Summer looked at her watch. 'We should head back,' she said, bringing Jude reluctantly back to reality. She stood up, then gasped. 'Oh shit! Jude, look! The tide's come in! Over the path! I think we're stuck!'

'You're kidding me . . . You don't think . . . Oh Summer, you don't think the siren was a warning signal, do you? Come to think of it, there were massive signs up just before the pathway warning about the tide. I haven't been paying attention.'

'What are we going to do? Will the sea reach us here? Have you got a phone on you? I didn't bring mine. We could call for help . . .'

'I left it in the car, but we'll be okay up here,' Jude told her. 'The tide can't come up this high. Though we'll be here for a little while.'

'How long? I'm sorry – I don't know anything about tides!'

'I don't know. I guess about six hours . . .'

'Six hours!'

'Unless someone sees us here before then. We'll have to keep our eyes peeled and wave for help if we see any boats or anything.'

'Oh, I'm so sorry, Jude. I shouldn't have dragged you down here. I'm wasting six of your precious hours!'

Jude didn't want to freak Summer out by telling her that they'd probably be the best six hours he'd spent in his entire life.

Chapter Fourteen

Jersey, Saturday

Summer

'I can understand that,' Summer said. She and Jude were sitting against a wall, trying to hide from the wind, which seemed to have picked up further with the change of tide. They were distracting themselves by talking. It seemed like the only thing to do to while away the time.

'You can? It felt like such a cop-out, leaving teaching just because of what happened with one student.'

'It was a big deal! You were badly hurt – physically and emotionally. Your heart wasn't in it any more. You can't do a job like that without your heart being in it. My mum was my teacher and I always knew she was one hundred per cent committed. I didn't go to school.'

'You're joking!'

'No, seriously. My parents are old hippies. We travelled around all through my childhood so my mum just home-schooled me. And before you say anything, no, I'm not scarred for life by my strange upbringing!'

'I was going to say that sounds wonderful! I never liked school much.'

'So what made you become a teacher then?'

'It was because of Mrs Carter. I had a huge crush on her. We all did. She was our English teacher in sixth form. But as well as being absurdly attractive, she was captivating when she discussed her subject. She sparked in me, for the first time, a genuine interest in learning and reading. I wanted to be like that. It sounds really lame, but I wanted to try to make a difference.'

'It's not lame at all. It's wonderful to be so optimistic.'

'Well, I was back then. Life's changed me.'

'It has a habit of doing that. But change is good. Change keeps us fresh.'

'I didn't feel fresh until the diagnosis. I felt jaded. But now . . . well, life just feels so different. There was this old chap I got talking to at the hospital who really brought it all home to me. I mean, obviously life is an amazing gift, but it's like I've only just realised how much I've been *squandering* it. That's a Daisy word. My sister.'

'You have siblings?'

'Just the one.'

'I'd have loved that. I'm an only child. I have twin boys and I've always been glad for them that they have each other.'

'How old are they?'

'Twenty!'

Jude raised his eyebrows. 'You must have been about fourteen when you had them!'

'Don't be silly,' Summer laughed. 'I was eighteen!'

'But so young . . . Is that why you got married?'

'Yes . . . a shotgun wedding. I guess it's amazing it's lasted this long.'

Jude looked like he was about to reply when Summer saw his eyes fix on something in the distance. 'Look!' he said, pointing. 'The coastguards! Someone must have seen us and given them a call. I guess we'd better wave to them.'

'Thank goodness!' Summer said. But as she was helped on to the boat she realised that, while relieved they were heading back to the safety and warmth of dry land, she was surprisingly sorry that she would never see this man – this attractive, dying man – again.

Summer was back at Mandla but she couldn't settle. She couldn't stop thinking about Jude's face when they'd said goodbye after he'd driven her along the road to Sylvie's. It was funny, but she'd thought he'd looked almost like he was about to cry when he'd reached across to the passenger seat to kiss her cheek. She'd felt quite emotional herself. 'Goodbye,' he'd said in a husky voice.

'Bye, Jude,' Summer had replied, a lump in her throat. She'd unlocked the front door and then turned back, thinking she should have invited him in for a drink, but his car had gone.

Summer was pacing the living room, nibbling her nails, when the house phone rang, making her jump.

'Hello?' she answered, expecting it to be for Sylvie.

'Hoorah, I've got you. I tried you a couple of times today!' It was Tilly. 'Where've you been?' she asked.

Summer told her the whole saga.

'Good heavens, what adventures you're having! And I'm sorry to have to tell you this, but you're not the only one. I'm afraid Seth's having an affair. I wanted to tell you the other day but I was interrupted by the postman.'

Summer was shocked. She sat down on a nearby chair with a thud. 'And that's the reason he wanted a break? But why not just end it completely? Are you sure?'

'I'm positive. I saw him in the churchyard, getting very frisky with Barbara Robinson.'

'Barbara! But she's at least ten years older than him! I'd have thought it'd be someone like that pretty young French teacher if anyone!'

'I know, it's absurd, but I *have* heard tales about her.'

'What sort of tales?'

'Oh, you don't want to know!'

'Yes I do!'

Tilly sighed. 'Let's just say she has a reputation for being rather *adventurous* in the bedroom. Ever since she and Reg divorced, she's been rampant. Up until now she's been using dating sites but . . . well . . .'

'Now she's sunk her teeth into Seth. Did he realise that you'd seen them?'

'Oh yes! He came round to see me later in the day. He didn't even deny it. But he begged me not to tell you.'

'Well, I'm glad you did.'

'Are you going to speak to him?'

Summer thought about it. 'No. No – we had a pact not to speak for six months and I'm going to stick to that. What he gets up to in that time . . . Well, let's just say we'll deal with it all after the break is over.'

They said their goodbyes, Tilly full of apologies, but Summer was actually grateful. After all, if Seth was having an affair, it put everything into a different perspective. She found her mobile and typed out a message.

It was really good to meet you today, Jude. I still can't believe the tide caught us out like that! If you fancy meeting up for a drink or something to eat some time, let me know . . . (And I can tell you're an honourable guy, so just so you know – I've found out my husband's having an affair.)

Too much information? Summer hesitated, but before she could have second thoughts she pressed 'send'. She received a reply less than a minute later. She smiled ruefully as she realised poor Jude didn't have time for the usual dating rules. It was great to meet you too! How about I take you out for dinner tomorrow night? To say thank you.

Thank you for what? Summer replied.

For making me feel alive.

Chapter Fifteen

Jersey, Sunday

Jude

Jude was agonising over where to take Summer for dinner. She didn't seem like the sort of person who would enjoy anywhere too fancy, and yet there was an understated sophistication about her – perhaps the result of her bohemian upbringing – that made him immediately discount any of the chain restaurants. In the end he rang Eddie for advice.

'Pizza Express?' he suggested.

'No, it's a chain. She's too free-spirited.'

Eddie laughed. 'What kind of food does she like?'

Jude racked his brains. 'She said she was into healthy eating usually, but she devoured all the biscuits I took to the lighthouse. And I think she said she was a pescatarian . . .'

'You mean she only eats fish?' Eddie asked, sounding aghast.

'Don't be stupid. It's like a vegetarian so they don't eat meat but they do eat fish.'

'Is she a hippy?' Eddie sounded wary.

'Not exactly. Her parents are but she's . . . she's just amazing.'

'Well, she must be – I've never known you to act like this. Look, mate, why don't you just take her to that little café down on the beach at La Pulente where you can bring your own booze. Nice and relaxed, you can watch the sun set. If the date's a disaster you don't have to stay long.'

'It's not really a date.'

'Yeah, whatever,' Eddie said disbelievingly. 'Have fun, won't you, and Cat says she wants a full report tomorrow.'

Jude smiled. 'Tell her I doubt there'll be much to report. Thanks for the advice – I hadn't thought of it, but it's perfect.'

'No worries, have a good one.'

The next problem was what to wear. Then Jude remembered about all his new clothes and was suddenly grateful to Daisy for frogmarching him round London. He picked out some nice jeans that – while brand new – looked suitably worn and faded, and a checked Superdry shirt that put him in mind of barn dances, but which Daisy had assured him was just right for 'casual'.

He arrived five minutes early, carrying a cooler bag full of alcohol. He hadn't known what Summer might like to drink so he'd covered all areas with champagne, white wine and some bottles of beer. He hadn't expected Summer to be there yet but he spotted her as soon as he made his way down the slipway. She was sitting at a picnic table wearing some kind of cute little mini-dress, playing with her necklace and staring out to sea. The sight of her made him catch his breath.

'The sun was just about to set,' she said as Jude approached. 'Then a cloud covered it over! It's still beautiful, though.'

'So are you,' Jude said, forgetting his promise to himself to play it cool. He thought Summer would laugh off his remark, embarrassed, but she leant forward and kissed his cheek, lingering slightly before leaning back again. The kiss would have looked like a completely run-of-the-mill greeting kiss to anyone looking at them, and yet Jude felt something ignite between them – a chemistry that could only possibly be felt and not explained. All his senses suddenly sharpened. The beach scene in front of him was like something from a Jack Vettriano picture. He could smell frying garlic wafting in their direction, making his mouth water. The sound of the waves on an incoming tide seemed clear and loud; the first sip of his beer tasted like nectar. And Summer's touch, when she reached out to take a beer from him and their hands accidentally brushed (he noticed she was no longer wearing her wedding ring), was . . . indefinable.

'I'm sorry,' Summer said, after the clash of hands. 'Actually, I'm not,' she amended. 'That feeling – your hand, my hand. It's like when you're wearing rubber soles on your shoes and closing the car door gives you a tiny electric shock.'

Not indefinable after all. She was exactly right. After that the food became unimportant, though it turned out to be delicious. Having scraped their plates clean and drunk all the beer, Summer said it was time she headed back to Mandla.

'It's a nice name for a house – Mandla,' Jude remarked.

'It's named after a favourite place of my aunt's in India. Her spiritual home. It's only round the corner, as you know. Do you want to walk back with me and get a cab home from there? We could have coffee?'

'I'd love to,' agreed Jude, and they started to make their way up from the beach, Jude using his phone as a torch.

Within ten minutes they'd reached the cottage and, once inside, Summer busied herself making the drinks while Jude went through to the living room. Summer joined him with the mugs and found him rifling through Sylvie's CDs.

'Hazel O'Connor. I haven't listened to her for years. My mum loves her.'

'Put it on,' Summer said, sitting down on one of the sofas. She started to sip her tea while Jude drank his coffee on the floor beside the stereo, then – listening to the words of 'Will You?' – they smiled slowly at each other. By the time the song reached the saxophone interlude, their drinks had been abandoned.

Jude felt a moment of nerves when their lips met. It had been a long while since he'd last had any physical relationship with anyone. He wondered if Summer felt as anxious as him.

'It . . . it's been a while,' Jude said, feeling embarrassed.

'Me too,' Summer murmured. 'I haven't had sex for a year. I guess I should have realised sooner that things weren't that great with Seth.'

'So we're both like born-again virgins,' Jude smiled, unbuttoning his shirt. He saw Summer's eyes clock the scar on his stomach where he'd been stabbed and felt self-conscious.

But, 'I'm sure we'll manage,' Summer replied, reaching out to touch his scar gently. 'And if it's a disaster, we'll just try again.'

Jude laughed, but it turned out it wasn't a disaster at all, and when he came across the three-quarter-full mugs the following morning, one of them with Summer's pendant looped around it, he knew for certain that he'd fallen well and truly in love.

Chapter Sixteen

Summer had expected to feel guilty after being with Jude but there was something that felt so absolutely right about their connection that she simply didn't. She would have done, she was sure, if she hadn't known about Barbara, but – as it was – it seemed fair enough.

She'd observed Jude over breakfast the following morning, already completely smitten as she admired how lovely his face looked so early in the day. She had a real thing about his eyebrows. They were naturally such a great shape – thick but not heavy, and brownish-blonde.

'What are you doing today?' she'd asked, watching him deftly peel a mango and cut it into neat slices.

'Flat-hunting,' he'd told her.

'What's wrong with your current place?'

'Nothing, really, but I've always wanted to live by the sea and if I want to achieve that life goal then I need to get on with it. The only problem is, there's not that much around at the moment. But we'll see – maybe I'll be able to find something close to Mandla!'

Summer, reverting to the naturally impulsive nature she'd tamed pretty well over the last twenty years, had taken hold of Jude's hand.

'Why don't you move in with me?' she'd said, and Jude had raised those beautiful eyebrows.

'Seriously?'

'Look, I know it's not sensible, but we're not dealing with normal timescales here, are we? And it makes sense if you're looking to move somewhere by the sea. I've got this place for at least six months.'

Jude had looked at Summer thoughtfully. 'What an incredibly generous offer . . . But are you sure your aunt won't mind? Do you need to speak to her?'

Summer had shaken her head. 'No, she won't mind at all . . . She's a complete free spirit. If it makes you feel better, why don't we try it out for a week or so and see how it goes?'

But already, after a week living together, they'd quickly established a happy routine – a slow and uncomplicated kind of regime.

Each day began with one of Summer's healthy breakfasts – a fruit smoothie, fresh fruit salad and Bircher muesli. Jude had baulked at the muesli initially but he'd been forced to admit it was very tasty. After breakfast, usually eaten on the terrace while reading the papers, they would walk for miles. But wherever they went they always tried to end up at a vegetarian café on the cliffs (fashionably named 'Veganista'), which was only ten minutes from the cottage.

Here they'd enjoy lunch before winding their way along the headland and down the steps to the cottage. They would go to bed together and then, while Jude rested, Summer would sit at the desk in the living room and try not to spend too long gazing out of the window as she got on with her magazine work. This done, she would turn off her laptop and set about creating an evening meal. She'd realised that, actually, if she stuck to food she was interested in eating herself she wasn't such a bad chef after all. It had been the endless meaty meals she'd prepared for Seth over the years that had challenged her, as well as all the sugary puddings he'd enjoyed. Assisted by the heat of the early summer, she and Jude stuck mainly to inventive salads – not Jude's first choice but he'd admitted he was a worse cook than Summer and was more than happy to just enjoy being fed, whatever the food.

And while all her food choices were healthy, Summer was as eager as Jude to enjoy a few drinks with their meals. He would drive up to Waitrose in St Brelade and cram his trolley with all kinds of beers and wine and stagger in with boxes of the stuff. Before the sun set they would sit out on the terrace on the wooden furniture enjoying a couple of beers and sometimes – if it was warm enough – eating out there.

Then, when it became too cold, they'd return to the warmth of the living room and sit on the floor playing Sylvie's board games – Scrabble and Snakes and Ladders and Guess Who?, an ancient children's game they both remembered playing as kids. Jude told Summer about an office version he and his colleagues had played during rainy lunch breaks.

'How did it work?' Summer asked.

'One player chose a person whose details were on the department phone list and they'd give "yes" or "no" answers to questions the other players asked while they tried to work out who the chosen colleague was.'

'What kind of questions?'

'Just like the board game, but with more personal details. You know – *Are they male? Yes. Do they have a moustache? Yes. Are they a complete dick? Yes. Is it Bradley Smith? Yes!*' Summer laughed.

It was all very simple and undemanding – exactly what they both needed.

One day – a particularly bright but breezy day – they went on an especially long walk, five miles along St Ouen's Bay from one end to the other, then past a series of potato fields where workers had arranged themselves in diagonal lines, industriously picking Jersey Royals. Then up the cliff steps at L'Etacq towards Grosnez, where they paused to take in the insanely beautiful mix of coast and agriculture. On the way back they retraced their steps but stopped off at Faulkner Fisheries – an old German bunker from the days of the occupation that had been turned into a fish shop. They'd only intended to buy some fish for their supper, which they did (some delicious-looking sea bass), but they spotted the owner lighting a barbecue.

'Staying for lunch?' the man asked. 'You just choose whatever you want and I'll throw it on the barbecue for you. There's beer and wine for sale, too, if you want a drink.' They did. They sat at a picnic bench and enjoyed a leisurely, boozy lunch while they ate fresh barbecued prawns and put the world to rights. They still had more than five miles to walk after this, stopping only briefly to buy potatoes from an honesty stall, and by the time they neared the cottage the bright sun had been replaced with dark clouds whipping in from the east. With a mile still to go, it began to pour with rain. Jude and Summer looked at each other and started to laugh wildly, then run, the bag of potatoes bouncing against Jude's hip. They arrived at the cottage drenched and exhilarated.

'Look at me! I've got to get out of these clothes,' Summer giggled. They were stuck to her like glue.

'Let me help,' said Jude, and he peeled off Summer's jeans then began tearing off his own as they started to kiss. The wet clothes abandoned on the cottage floor, they ended up in bed. Afterwards they rested, contented. Jude was quiet.

'You okay?' Summer asked him, conscious that he could easily slip from feeling well to terrible when his headaches struck.

'I'm fine,' he told her. 'Just thinking.'

'About?'

'My bucket list.'

'No way! I've heard of those. Fifty things you want to do before you die – that kind of thing? Have you always had one?'

'Nope. It was something I came up with after I was diagnosed. I thought the list would help me achieve a few things. Not fifty things – just a handful – and they're pretty unambitious. My parents brought me up to value the simple things in life, although there *are* two items on the list that I'm too curious not to try. Staying in a five-star hotel and driving a flashy car! I want to know what all the fuss is about!'

'What else?' asked Summer, curious.

Jude smiled sheepishly. 'Well, number one on the list is not to die alone.'

Summer felt tears spring to her eyes. 'Surely that would never happen? Your family . . .'

'I know I can count on them. I guess I was hoping I might meet someone who would stick by me and be with me to the end . . .'

'And you have!'

'Let's not jump the gun. It's early days still.'

'I mean it, Jude,' Summer said, still feeling emotional. 'What else is on the list?' she asked, trying to fight back tears. 'We should get started on it!'

'I'd love to, but before I make a start on ticking off the things on the bucket list I want to find out more about my grandmother.'

'What do you mean?'

'She lived through the Nazi occupation of Jersey and when she was alive I never really asked her about it. I don't know why but it suddenly feels important – to find out what she lived through. I could ask my parents but I'm trying to avoid talking to them – I don't feel ready to burden them with my news. I've managed to track down one of Granny Sabine's old friends. She's still in Jersey – in a nursing home. I was planning to go and visit her. Would you . . . I mean, would you find it dreadfully boring to come with me?'

'I'd love to!' Summer told him. 'This is turning out to be quite an adventure. I was picturing six months of dossing around on my own doing very little, and now look at me!'

'You don't look like a layabout anyway!' Jude laughed. 'But you must tell me if you want some time alone. Please just say, won't you?'

'I will. But for now, let's set things in motion with this lady. I can't wait to meet her . . .'

'I'll sort something out. Sooner rather than later.'

Summer smiled, both the journalist and humanist in her intrigued to find out more about this woman who'd lived through the Nazi occupation with Jude's grandmother.

Chapter Seventeen

JERSEY

JUDE

'It's down this lane, I think,' said Summer, scanning the map. 'Yes, look – there's a sign – the Willow Lane Nursing Home.' Jude indicated and turned left and two minutes later they were pulling up in front of a large, impersonal-looking building.

'I'd hate to end up somewhere like this,' Summer said as she unfastened her seatbelt. 'Like an orphanage for old people.'

'Luckily, I'm not going to have that problem!' laughed Jude, but Summer just looked sad. 'Come on, you,' he said the next moment, pulling her out of the passenger seat.

Having signed in and been led along endless corridors by a severe-looking woman with dyed black hair, they finally met the reason for their visit: Di. She was instantly fascinating – 102 years old and yet sitting in an armchair looking immaculate. She had long silver hair, a dainty bone structure and an incredibly warm and smiling face.

'Well, what a treat this is!' Di told them immediately in her charming cockney accent. She'd lived in Jersey for most of her adult life but she'd never lost the accent. 'Come and sit down 'ere. Would you like a cuppa?' she asked. Jude and Summer said they would.

'Jilly!' she called back to the severe lady. 'Three cups of tea and a plate of your finest biscuits, please!' she ordered, as though in a smart five-star hotel rather than a somewhat gloomy residential home.

Jilly looked like she might argue but thought better of it and returned five minutes later with a stainless-steel pot of tea, three pale-green 1940s teacups and a plate of bourbons.

'I don't believe these are the finest they can muster,' Di muttered before Jilly was out of earshot, 'but I 'ope they'll do?' she smiled.

'Of course! I love bourbons,' said Summer, and Jude looked on in amusement as she started to scoff the biscuits, just as she had the first time they'd met.

'Now,' Di said, appraising Jude fully. 'Well, aren't you a toothsome young boy! Dear me, you'd 'ave been just my type three-quarters of a century ago,' she chuckled. 'But then your grandmother was an 'and-some woman. One of my best friends she turned out to be – Sabine. I still miss 'er now. I weren't 'alf sad when she passed away. We first got to know each other during the occupation years.'

'How did you meet?'

'I moved to Jersey after I married me first 'usband – we met in London but Jersey was 'is 'ome. Well, 'e turned out to be a rotter, that man, but I 'ad me kids with 'im so I couldn't regret nothing. Then 'e died of an 'eart attack – 'e weren't even thirty! That was before the war started. I was just about able to make ends meet, got meself a job as a seamstress. Then next thing we knew there was a rumour the Jerries were 'eading to Jersey! I packed me kids off to stay with a cousin in London and I was going to follow after, once I got the 'ouse sorted out. Only before I got a chance, the Germans 'ad invaded and then in 1942 I was deported to an internment camp in Germany. Five years I didn't see my nippers. They barely recognised me when I finally saw 'em again.

Broke my 'eart, that did.' Di paused, deeply sad at the remembrance, and Summer reached out to hold her wizened hand.

'I didn't know what to do with meself, but there was this pantomime going on. The second Christmas of the occupation. I was asked to make the costumes and that kept me nice and busy. That was when I met your gran. Sabine. She was playing Cinderella. She were great friends with a girl called Queenie and they was a bit younger than me, but ever such nice girls. After I was sent off to the camp in Germany I 'ad no way to keep in touch with 'em. But after the war I remarried and went to live in the north of England – and then, a few years later, I moved back to Jersey with me second 'usband, Glen – he was a goody, that one, though he went and died before me 'n' all. So we made Jersey our 'ome back in the fifties. That was when I met up with Sabine again and we became very friendly. She'd just 'ad a baby when I moved back – your mum, Beryl – and I 'elped 'er out, gave 'er a bit of advice.'

'I can't imagine what it must have been like living here when the island was taken over. Was it a shock?' Summer asked.

'Well, it was and it wasn't. The Germans 'ad defeated France and we're such close neighbours we knew it would just be a matter of time, but we kept 'olding out 'ope that the British would somehow find a way to protect us. Most of us 'ad been burying our 'eads in the sand but in June 1940 we were told the island was going to be "demilitarised" or whatever they called it and we 'ad to decide whether to evacuate or not. There was an awful lot of dithering and talking. When German aircraft started flying over, more and more people began to flee. A woman along the road from us 'ot-footed it down to the 'arbour one day 'alfway through 'er ironing – she left the iron on in 'er fluster and the 'ouse set fire! That was when I sent the kids off, thinking I could follow later. A mistake, that was, although at least they were spared being packed off to Germany.'

'So what was it like – after the invasion?' asked Jude as he sipped his tea.

'At the start, it weren't too bad. The soldiers we came across at that stage were mostly young and not too intimidating, aside from the air force officers. My word, they were an arrogant lot! Attractive enough, but far too full of themselves. Then they disappeared all of a sudden and it were just the ground soldiers left. Well, them and the Gestapo, of course. After the war ended everyone said there 'adn't been any Gestapo in Jersey during the occupation but if you ask me there was! After the invasion, at first we was able to go about our lives reasonably normally aside from a lot of silly rules. But the Gestapo, or whoever they were, put the fear into you. Worst kind of eavesdroppers, they were! You soon learnt just to pass the time of day with friends when you saw 'em in the street, as you could never be sure who was listening.'

'What kind of rules were there?' asked Summer.

'Some were just plain daft, but others were more serious – they banned wirelesses. Didn't want anyone listening to the British news broadcasts. So everyone 'ad to 'and over their sets, although some people 'ad a couple and 'anded in one and kept the other 'idden. If anyone got caught with a wireless after the ban, they risked being packed off to a concentration camp in Europe. You 'ad to be so careful – there were neighbours settling grievances by grassing on their old rivals. But the news broadcasts were an obsession for everyone. To be without a wireless made 'em feel like there was no 'ope. Like I say, I was packed off to Germany in 1942, but after the war ended I found out what Sabine 'ad been up to. She'd taken terrible risks as the war 'ad gone on: braver and braver she'd got as time went by. She were very close to the organist in our local church and persuaded 'im to let 'er keep a wireless 'idden under the floorboards next to the organ. She'd go into the church, often after curfew, and listen to the news. The penalties got 'arsher and 'arsher, but she carried on. She even started up a news-sheet that was passed around the island.

She was never caught, though she came close a couple of times. She was brave, that girl. Brave or foolish, I said to 'er when she told me what she'd been up to during those years.'

'I didn't know this!' Jude exclaimed, pouring more tea. 'I mean, she'd occasionally tell me a few tales about Jersey in wartime, but she never told me that.'

'Well, she learnt to be secretive. We all did. Probably didn't want to brag, neither. It weren't the only brave thing she did. But in a way, I always thought the drowning incident were the most courageous thing of all.'

'She nearly drowned?' asked Jude.

'Not 'er. She was a very strong swimmer. I was, too. In fact, I saved my Glen when 'e got tangled up in 'is parachute at St Brelade's Bay, but that's another story. Sabine saved a German soldier, down at 'avre des Pas, quite early on in the occupation. He was a young lad – about our age. We thought 'e was mucking about but then Sabine realised 'e was drowning. He'd gone out too far and the current was strong. He was panicking, flailing about. She didn't think twice. She plunged into the sea and swam out to 'im, saved his life. She saw 'im as another 'uman being when most of us that day would've just left the enemy to drown. Her actions were frowned upon by some. She were accused of fraternising with the enemy. But Sabine weren't one of those Jerry-bags who took off with the soldiers, then lorded it over the rest of us. The soldier did become almost a friend to Sabine, though, after she saved 'im. He became a useful ally at times. Anyway, that was Sabine. Brave, through and through.'

'It's all so interesting,' Summer remarked. 'I just can't believe how different it must have been.'

'Oh, it was! The deprivations. Sabine said she thought they'd all starve to death by the end. But she told me as well about the celebrations when the island were freed! The ninth of May 1945. Sabine and 'er friend Queenie watched the Nazi flag being taken down from the

Pomme d'Or Hotel – that nasty swastika – and replaced with the Union Jack. She said she'd never forget that day!'

Di paused, as if in a reverie, and Jude and Summer were reluctant to disturb her. Eventually she shook her head. 'I've gone on, I'm sorry, and now me tea is cold!'

'Let me go and get some more,' Summer said. 'And then we should probably go. We don't want to outstay our welcome.'

'Now that would be impossible!' Di said. 'But I 'aven't found out anything about the pair of you! Will you come again?' she asked, and all at once she seemed her age. Vulnerable. Lonely. 'Only me kids both live abroad now – me girl's in New Zealand and me boy's in California. They visit now and then, but they're getting quite frail themselves . . .'

'Of course we will,' promised Summer. 'Is there anything we can bring you?'

Di thought for a moment. 'Mango!' she said with a big smile. 'Oh, 'ow I miss mango! They never give us any exotic fruit in 'ere.'

'We'll bring you mango!' Jude promised.

Summer and Jude made sure to visit once a week after that, always bringing a perfectly ripe mango with them, which Jude dexterously peeled and chopped for Di with a penknife. He sometimes recorded Di's tales on his phone, too, so that he could play them back later, immersing himself in his family history as though he were going to be tested on it by his grandmother as soon as he made it through the Pearly Gates.

'There's so much to learn about, so much to know . . . It's like I've only just realised,' Jude explained to Summer one evening, clearly agitated. 'I feel like I'm running out of time. How am I going to make sure I do everything – learn everything? Time's slipping through my fingers like sand.'

'You have to try not to panic,' Summer said, gently stopping Jude as he paced up and down the living room. 'If you panic you won't enjoy it, and that's the aim, isn't it? Quality, not quantity?' But her words fell on deaf ears and in the end she went to bed alone while Jude continued to pace.

Eventually he downed a large glass of brandy, then went to bed, where he slept not the sleep of the dead, but the twitchy, panicky, fruitless sleep of the dying.

Chapter Eighteen

Jersey

Summer

A few weeks after they first met Di, Jude and Summer decided to take her out for afternoon tea. Jude's panicky phase seemed to have subsided, thanks to Summer's patience and reassurance, and he was looking more relaxed than he had in a while.

Di was thoroughly enjoying a rare outing and had been regaling them with more tales about Sabine. This time about the work she did for women's rights in the years following the war, as well as more stories of her innate bravery during the years of the occupation.

'Sabine's mother – your great-grandmother, Odette – was an incredibly strong woman. You might 'ave imagined that, running an 'air salon – as she did in the thirties and forties – she would 'ave only been interested in making women look good. But she was a real feminist. She refused to take part in the 1911 census. Women 'adn't been given the right to vote in Britain or the Channel Islands at that time and the suffragettes decided to protest by staying out the night when the census was taken or refusing to complete it, just writing their complaints on the form instead. It weren't until 1919 that women were able to vote in Jersey, a year after the UK. She were ever so modern, Odette, and she 'ad Sabine quite late in life, like mothers do nowadays. It rubbed off on Sabine – during the war the entire population was suppressed, but afterwards she campaigned for women's rights in an era that was particularly focused on family and 'ome. The forties and fifties were tricky times to be a woman. It weren't an easy ride and she ended up moving to England to join up with like-minded women there for a while. She only moved back to Jersey later, just before I did, when she married and 'ad your mother and her sister. Are they feminists too? I always wondered about that.'

Jude looked like he was thinking about the question for a moment. 'I'm not sure about Auntie Irene. But my mum, Beryl, seems the oppo-site of a feminist at first glance – a cosy, stay-at-home mother with no interest in a career. But she never lets my father get away with any prejudice against women in conversation, so I suppose, in her own way, she is. And she was very adamant that Daisy should make a career for herself. In fact, when you talk about Odette and Sabine, it sounds like you're talking about my sister. I know now where she got her spark from.'

Di smiled, but she was looking tired. 'I might just close me eyes for a few moments. Do you mind?' Jude shook his head and Summer poured more tea. Moments later, Di was dozing in her chair while they chatted quietly.

'It's quite amazing,' breathed Summer. 'I'm blown away by all these stories. It makes me a bit embarrassed about how much I've tried to be the perfect headmaster's wife for Seth. I'm a free spirit at heart and I let him, and my role, change me.'

'But not permanently,' Jude remarked.

'No,' Summer smiled. 'Only a twenty-year blip . . .'

They were enjoying their tea in the grounds of Longueville Manor, the only sound the chirruping of birds pecking at the leftover crumbs beside their outdoor table, the sun catching the emerald in Summer's necklace so that it shone. Jude was intrigued by this piece of jewellery Summer wore every day, without fail – a silver pendant with two hands reaching towards the emerald in the middle. He wanted to ask her if Seth had given it to her, but dreaded the answer.

'Do you think you're a feminist at heart? Despite trying to be the perfect headmaster's wife?' asked Jude.

'I've always felt it sounds somehow derogatory, that word. My mother, Vita, is a true feminist – she was burning her bras back in the sixties. It would have been impossible for some of that not to influence me. I'd say I'm a quiet feminist. Don't get me started on equal pay, for example! How is it justified in this day and age for a man to be paid more than a woman for doing exactly the same job?' Summer stopped and smiled. 'Actually, once I get started I can get quite irate.'

'I don't blame you. And I think I'm a feminist myself, although as a man you don't admit that to too many people. Perhaps a better word is an egalitarian. Equality. Maybe one day . . .'

'Hmmm, maybe. But your grandmother. How incredible she sounds. But perhaps not so surprising, knowing you as I now do. A quiet warrior, that's what you are.'

'Me?' asked Jude, his face shocked. 'Summer, I've never done anything brave in my life. I'm the complete opposite to my granny.'

'That's not true – you chased down that student who stabbed you. And look at how you're dealing with a terminal illness,' Summer whispered. 'Jude, you don't know it, but you're every bit as brave as your grandmother. You're the most courageous person I know.'

She looked at Jude, to try to work out if he believed in his bravery yet himself, but she could see in his eyes that – even now – he didn't agree with her.

Chapter Nineteen

JUDE'S BUCKET LIST:

2. LEARN TO SURF

The day after their afternoon tea, Jude decided to tackle his bucket list, thinking they should focus on something fun in the wake of his period of panic about the short time he had left. Summer had been incredibly patient but he wanted their relationship to go back to being fresh and fun, as it had been just after they'd met – not burdened with his woes.

'Have either of you surfed before?' asked the Aussie surf instructor, Chaz, who was tall, bronzed and muscly. He was the definition of 'cool' and Jude felt instantly dorky in his rather too-tight wetsuit. It felt like it was choking him.

'No,' he answered in a slightly strangled tone.

'Me neither,' said Summer. 'But I'm so excited.'

'You both swim though, right?' asked Chaz, a frown momentarily crossing his perfect features.

'Oh yes,' agreed Summer, breezily. 'Shall we get started?'

They began with some instructions on dry land, lying on their boards, making paddling motions with their arms, and then trying to get the hang of pushing up and springing to their feet. This all seemed fairly pointless to Jude. Surely it would be completely different on the water? But he'd always been a good student and he wasn't going to start rebelling now. After a slightly tedious half an hour on the beach, they were finally told to follow Chaz into the water up to their waists. It was icy, even at this time of year and in a wetsuit, and after a couple of minutes Jude could no longer feel his feet. Summer's lips went blue.

'You'll warm up soon enough once you start moving,' Chaz assured them, shouting above the splash of the white water. They spent some time chest-deep in water, catching the broken waves and trying to stand up on their boards. After both Jude and Summer had managed this a couple of times, Jude shouted towards Chaz.

'Mate, can we go in a bit deeper?' he asked boldly, determined to test his bravery with this challenge.

Chaz looked a bit uncertain but he agreed. 'Okay, we'll paddle out a bit deeper – out the back, into the green waves. But guys, you really need to use your chest and arms for this bit. Put a bit of welly into it.' They did their best and eventually reached Chaz, who'd quickly paddled out. Jude was exhausted already – probably more down to lack of fitness than anything to do with his illness, he had to admit to himself.

'Here's a big one coming in,' Chaz said, scanning the horizon. 'So remember, you want to jump up on to the board just before the wave rolls in then get your balance and you're off.'

He made it sound so simple. It wasn't. Jude and Summer wibbled, wobbled, were battered around and swallowed a huge amount of sea water. They didn't catch a single wave but they laughed a hell of a lot – both rather pleased that at least the other wasn't excelling.

'Right, guys, there's a bit of a rip developing – can you feel the pull? I think we'd better head in . . .' But Chaz was too late and all of a sudden their laughter only moments before seemed absurd. They could feel the water sucking them out to sea and no amount of paddling was making any difference. It was strange because, even though Jude stared death in the face on a daily basis, this danger felt far more immediate and – as a consequence – quite terrifying.

'Shit, I've never had this happen before,' Chaz told them. He was looking panicked, which wasn't reassuring. 'We're going to have to let the current take us out and then paddle out of it alongside the shore once it settles down. But if you see a wave coming in you've got to try to catch it into the beach.'

Seeing as neither Jude nor Summer had managed to pick up a single wave so far, the idea of catching one into the beach didn't seem particularly realistic.

But a minute later Jude and Summer saw a roller approaching. A big one. They looked at each other, understanding passing between them. *This is it*, the look said. *We do this and we do it together.* Just as the wave reached them, Jude and Summer paddled their boards towards the beach with an almost superhuman strength. The wave jacked up and they were tipped down its face as it broke, inelegantly clinging on to their boards for their lives and swallowing more water as the frothing wave bumped them around. Neither of them knew how long their one ride took, but they made it, crashing into each other as they fell from their boards and submerged. They pulled themselves out of the water. Shallow. But even here the rip was pulling hard. They staggered from the water on to the sand, both shaking now, and scanned the sea for Chaz. They saw him. He was coming, riding the next wave in perfectly. He waved.

'Bit of fun and games!' he grinned as he swaggered out of the water, composure recovered. 'I don't charge extra for that,' he told them. 'You did fantastic, though, guys. You gonna come back for another lesson tomorrow?'

Jude and Summer, still trembling, looked at each other, eyes wide. Jude shook his head. 'Think we'll take a rain check, but thanks, mate. It was fun,' he said weakly. They shook hands and Jude and Summer ran up the beach to the spot where Summer had left her bag, collapsing on to the softer sand and laughing hysterically – purging all their fear with tears of laughter.

'What on earth made you choose learning to surf?' Summer asked eventually as she peeled off her wetsuit.

'I had no idea it would be that difficult! My friend Eddie makes it look so easy! If I'm honest, I wanted to test myself physically – to see how I'd get on with a sport that requires a decent amount of upper-body strength. It hasn't exactly boosted my body confidence, but it was just as exhilarating as I'd hoped it would be. You can't tell me you're not feeling the endorphins after all that adrenaline!'

'That's true,' Summer agreed, drying herself with a towel. 'We survived it! And that feels good!'

'But it's also made me realise that perhaps I'm better off just accepting my limitations for now. I don't want to die even more prematurely than necessary.' Jude smiled ruefully but Summer didn't smile back. He knew she hated him to joke about his situation, but sometimes it felt like the only way to handle it.

Jude watched as she delved into her bag and then shrugged on one of her mini-dresses, before looping her necklace over her head and throwing one of his hoodies over the top.

'I love your dress,' he said. 'Those retro clothes really suit you.'

'Thanks,' Summer smiled. 'All the sixties and seventies clothes I've got were my mum's when she was young.'

'Ah, that explains it then. I thought they smelt a bit fusty when I found them in the case.'

'How embarrassing! I meant to wash them once I got here – I have now, of course. I used to wear those clothes as a teenager. They represent one of the happiest periods in my life. I probably look like a has-been in them, but they're just . . . Well, they're just sort of "me".'

'They are,' Jude agreed as he got dressed himself. 'They're totally you. A change from all the skinny jeans everyone seems to live in. You're beautiful in them.' Jude blushed, unused to giving compliments so naturally, and looked at the ground. Summer kissed him, then took his hand.

'Come on!' she said and, cocooned in their hoodies, they made their way up from the beach and sat outside the Watersplash bar for sundowners. Jude had told Summer about the incredible sunsets there and this one didn't disappoint. They sat together at a picnic table, looking out to sea, and drank bottles of beer as the sun began to dip in the sky. They looked scruffy, with damp hair full of sea salt and slightly sunburnt noses, but after the exhilaration of their surfing adventure – and their subsequent relief at not drowning – they felt almost euphoric.

'Have you got your phone?' asked Summer suddenly. 'Let's take a selfie, with the sunset in the background.'

Jude laughed. 'A selfie? You sound like you're part of the Suki generation.' Jude had been telling Summer all about Suki from his work the night before.

'It's my boys – they're forever taking them. Come on,' she said. They hopped over to the other side of the picnic bench so that the blood-red sun would be in the picture and Summer snuggled into Jude. 'You take it – you've got longer arms.'

He did. And by some stroke of genius he captured everything in that one shot. Joy. Laughter. Sadness. Friendship. Love. It was the only photo they took that summer – their time spent creating memories rather than recording them – but it was a picture Jude hoped Summer would treasure for ever.

Chapter Twenty

A Bad Day

Summer

Despite Jude's determination to focus on fun while they began to work through his bucket list, there were still good days and bad days for him as his illness progressed. This one was a bad one. He'd woken up looking pale beneath his tan.

'My head . . .' he groaned.

'Let me get your pills,' Summer said, jumping up and grabbing the tablets from the bathroom and a cool drink of water. 'Here you go,' she said, smoothing his hair back from his forehead and kissing it. He felt clammy. 'Do you want any breakfast?' she asked. She knew he hated her to fuss over him, but he clearly had no idea just how much she wanted to look after him. She might be a free spirit but she was also naturally nurturing and the love she felt for Jude made her desire to care for him unequivocal.

'No, no food. I'm so sorry – it's a bad day. Will you be okay?'

'Don't worry about me – I ought to get some work done anyway. I haven't done anything for days. I'm just sorry you feel so rubbish. Can I do anything else? Do you want me to call the consultant?'

'No point. He said this would happen. I'll be better by tomorrow.' He put a couple of enormous tablets in his mouth and washed them down, wincing, while Summer threw on some clothes.

Then she smoothed the covers over Jude as he lay back against the pillows, adjusted the blinds and left him to rest. She went through to the living room and sat on a sofa, fiddling anxiously with her necklace. Worry, worry, worry. But it wouldn't achieve anything, so she grabbed her purse and walked up the hill to the nearby honesty stall to see what vegetables were on offer. Everything she'd need for ratatouille – onions, garlic, herbs, tomatoes, courgettes and aubergines. She bought them then walked for a little longer as fast as she could – trying to expel her angst – before she returned to the cottage and started chopping up the vegetables, immersing herself in domesticity.

After a while Summer abandoned her preparation and went to check on Jude. He lay sleeping under the starched white covers, his head slightly propped by a square goose-down pillow. A small frown indicated that, though sleeping, his head still throbbed. Summer crept on to the bed and snuggled into him, listening to his heart steadily thumping beneath his T-shirt. She could hear the sounds of the radio drifting through from the kitchen. Coldplay's 'Adventure of a Lifetime', a favourite of the local radio station. After hearing it several times, they'd adopted it as their song.

It was a bit mainstream for Jude (so far, Summer had been introduced to the lesser-known likes of Gene, The Weird Ians and Feeder) but the lyrics rang true for them: they really did make each other feel alive again.

Summer began to cry silently, her tears soaking Jude's T-shirt. His heart sounded so strong and regular and *normal*. And yet he would die. Within a year. Summer had gently asked him about it a couple of days before.

'What will happen, Jude? I mean, when things get worse . . .'

'I'll start to sleep more,' he'd explained, gazing into his gin and tonic, not looking at her. 'I'll get drowsier and drowsier and eventually I'll slip into unconsciousness. I guess there are worse ways to go,' he'd mumbled.

Summer had jumped up from her chair and gone to stand behind him, putting her arms around him. She'd felt a heavy sadness dragging her down, though – as ever – she'd tried hard to be brave for him. 'I'll be there for you. Whenever it happens.'

'But what if your six-month break is over? Are you going back to your husband?'

'I've no idea, but I wasn't the one who made the six-month rule. I'm going to be here, right here, till the end. Making the most of every minute.' She'd barely been able to get the words out, the lump of emotion in her throat feeling as though it might choke her.

Jude's shoulders had started to shake and they'd both cried, then blamed the gin, then eventually gone to bed, where they'd made each other feel better. And the next day they hadn't talked about it any more. They'd made plans for the next item on the bucket list. But although they rarely discussed his disease, Summer had her private moments of deep despair and she was sure Jude had them too.

When she became afraid of waking Jude with her tears, Summer slipped from the bed and ran out of the cottage, down to the sea. She was fully clothed but she kept running – into the ocean – the salt water mixing with her tears. She sobbed loudly, the sound drowned out by the hum of the sea.

'It's just not fair!' she shouted out towards the lighthouse. And it wasn't. But there was nothing either of them could do about it.

Her sadness and fury eventually subsided, and Summer returned to the cottage, where she showered and changed. She returned to her cooking. Half an hour later, Jude found her.

'Smells amazing,' he said, smiling, his hair all rumpled.

'How are you feeling?' Summer asked.

'Better,' he told her. 'Much better.'

He went over to Summer and pulled her into a hug. She could hear his heart beating through his T-shirt, faster than before. He began singing the Coldplay song, then stopped.

'You were sad,' he mumbled into Summer's ear.

'Did I wake you?' she replied, concerned not only about disturbing him but also about burdening him with her own feelings when he already had so much to deal with.

'I was half-asleep but a little bit aware . . . You soaked my top! Oh Summer, I can't bear it. I don't ever want to leave you.'

Summer lost her battle to be brave – his words made her burst into tears again, noisy this time. She let them all out while Jude just hugged her tight.

Chapter Twenty-One

JUDE'S BUCKET LIST:

3. SEE MORE OF DAISY

'I'm going away,' Jude announced to Summer the following day.

Summer was busy hulling strawberries at the wooden table on the terrace. It was a blustery day so her hair was fluttering about, but it was warm enough. She looked up. 'Not for long, I hope?'

'Just a long weekend. When I was diagnosed, I promised Daisy I'd see more of her, and I've not been very available so far. I spoke to her last night when you were in the bath and promised I'd go over this weekend. She really wants to meet you, too, but I said I'd go on my own this time as she wants to have serious chats with me about various things.' Jude pulled a face. 'Daisy is an expert at yanking my head out of the sand. She's going to say that I need to tell my parents what's going on and, if I'm doing that, I need her by my side . . .'

'I'll miss you,' Summer said, shielding her eyes against the sun as she looked up at him.

'Me too,' Jude said, feeling an ache already at the thought of leaving her, though he knew it was the right thing to do.

This time Daisy met him at Gatwick Airport.

'You didn't have to,' Jude said as they hugged.

'I know, but Sam's at home and I wanted us to be able to have a chat just the two of us.'

'What about?' asked Jude, though he knew what she was going to say.

'Jude, you've got to tell Mum and Dad. It's just not right. Mum's in a fluster because you haven't been in touch for ages – she thinks she's upset you. And she keeps asking after you and I have to keep fibbing and telling her you're just fine when you're bloody well dying!'

Daisy looked just like she had as a child when she'd felt wronged: eyes bloodshot with imminent tears, her porcelain skin temporarily red, clashing with her hair.

'Dais! I'm sorry . . . Come here!' Jude hugged her again. 'I didn't think how it must be for you. I'm sorry . . . You're right. I've just been putting it off. I can't bear to do it to them. And, I admit, I'm struggling so much to process it all myself, I'm not sure I can handle having to deal with their feelings as well.'

Daisy was mollified. 'I know, I understand, but we'll do it together, Jude. We'll FaceTime them after lunch, okay? It'll be horrible, but then it'll be done.'

'It won't be done though, really, will it? It'll be the beginning for them.' Jude sighed. 'Can we at least have a drink first?' he asked.

'Just one!' Daisy bossed. 'We need to have our wits about us!'

That afternoon, Sam made herself scarce and Jude and Daisy set themselves up with Daisy's iPad.

'G'day!' beamed their father, showing off a terrible double chin, thanks to the unflattering angle at which he'd placed his own tablet.

'Dad, try putting the iPad up a bit, so we're not looking up your nostrils,' said Daisy, and there followed a lot of faffing about while he tried to reposition it.

'I'll do it, dear!' they heard Beryl say next and eventually they had a view of both of their double chins. They gave up.

'Jude! Where have you been? You're so naughty. We haven't heard from you in months!'

'I know. I'm sorry, Mum.'

'Well, what have you been up to?' she asked.

'I've met someone,' said Jude, thinking this would be a nice decoy from the purpose of the call.

'I knew it! Didn't I say that?' Beryl asked, turning her double chin towards her husband's. 'Didn't I say it would be a woman! Oh, I'm so pleased for you, Jude. Tell us all about her.'

'Okay . . . Well . . .' Jude began, relieved not to have to go into the depressing subject of his tumour, but Daisy interrupted.

'Actually, Mum, Jude has some difficult news for you both.' She prodded Jude and he sighed, resigned.

'Yes, um . . . Look, I'm really sorry about this, but I've . . . er, it turns out I've got a . . . a brain tumour,' Jude said, closing his eyes as he rubbed his eyebrows. 'It's a bad one. They can't operate to get rid of it . . . and the long and the short of it is, I'm . . . I'm going to die,' Jude mumbled, opening his eyes again. He tried to swallow the tears he could feel building and felt relieved at the terrible angle of the iPad, which at least prevented him from having a clear view of his parents' faces.

There was silence. Beryl and David looked at each other. Eventually, his father spoke. 'Jude, we're all going to die. The question is, when?'

'Less than a year.'

A sob shot out of his mother's mouth. 'No, no, no, no, no!' she wailed. 'No, not my baby. Not my baby boy!'

Daisy put her hands over her eyes. Jude felt like doing the same. It was too raw and painful to watch their mother's heart break, just like that – in the delivery of one garbled confession over FaceTime.

'I think we'd better call you back,' his father said, gulping. 'Don't go far. I'll just get your mother some tissues and a cup of tea.' Like everything would be solved with a blow of the nose and a hot drink. But it was clearly all the poor man could think to do.

'You call us back,' Daisy said. 'We'll be right here.'

They rang ten minutes later and the entire afternoon was spent FaceTiming, with intermittent comfort breaks. Daisy agreed to more alcohol now the dreadful news had been imparted and they all analysed the symptoms, the diagnosis, the potential for a misdiagnosis and the practicalities.

'We'll fly over, won't we, David?' Beryl said, looking towards her husband. 'We'll come tomorrow if need be.'

'There's no mad panic,' Jude told them. 'Dad, get everything sorted out with work and see what you can find on the flight front. I'm not going to keel over tomorrow. You'll need a bit of time to get everything sorted, especially if you're going to come over for a little while.'

'Yes,' said Beryl, and he could imagine her mind busily thinking about everything she'd need to organise. *Arrange the cattery for Bumble and Bee, ask Mary to water the plants, cancel the newspaper delivery, rearrange various socials . . .* 'Maybe if we tried to be with you in a couple of weeks' time? Would that be okay?' she asked, her voice still wobbly.

'Of course, Mum!'

By the time he went to bed that night, Jude felt drained, but he did what he'd wanted to do all day. He called up Summer.

'Jude! How's it all going?' she asked. 'It doesn't feel right here without you.'

'I miss you too – and Mandla. I've never known a place to feel so quickly like home.'

'Did you tell your parents?'

Jude sighed. 'Yes . . . I'm glad I've done it, but Summer, it was awful. To break their hearts like that. I feel so guilty.'

'It's hardly your fault,' Summer said comfortingly, 'but I can understand those feelings. They'll be in shock right now, but it's much better that they know. Are they going to travel over?'

'Yes, they're going to come to Jersey. I'm absolutely knackered now so I'll tell you all the details once I'm home. I just wanted to hear your voice before I go to sleep.'

'I'm glad you called,' Summer replied. 'You should sleep well tonight,' she said. 'You'll feel lighter now you've told your parents.'

Jude realised, as he drifted off to sleep, that Summer was right – telling his parents had been preying more heavily on his mind than he'd realised. It hadn't been any less painful than expected, but the worst was over. And soon, very soon, they'd be with him, giving him the steady comfort he'd known all his life. They'd given him that unconditional, all-encompassing comfort from the moment he was born and now, sadly, they'd be there to offer it when he died.

Chapter Twenty-Two

Jersey

Summer

It was strange, because Summer had been more than happy in her own company when she'd first arrived in Jersey. She'd been cock-a-hoop to enjoy sleeping, eating and reading alone in Sylvie's beautiful cottage.

But it wasn't the same. By Sunday she was well and truly moping for her man and the thought squeezed her stomach painfully as she realised she'd better get used to it. Horribly soon she would be alone and with no prospect of a happy reunion. She shook her head, trying to dispel such maudlin thoughts. And anyway, Jude would be home the following day. She just needed to focus on that.

Feeling a little lonely, that evening she decided to call Tilly. They'd barely spoken since she'd first arrived and she felt guilty. But there was no answer. She looked at her phone. She tried Levi and Luke next. Levi was out but Luke was interested in everything she'd been up to.

'I've met someone,' she told him honestly.

'I thought you would,' he replied.

'You didn't!'

'Look, Mum, it's clear things haven't been right between you and Dad for a while and you're still super-pretty and young. I thought – out of the two of you – it would be you who'd end up meeting someone else while you were on this break.'

'Actually, your dad's met someone too, apparently.'

'Really?' Luke seemed surprised. 'Who?'

'Barbara from the village!' Summer said, unable to contain her giggles.

'You're joking!' Luke laughed. 'Gah, I hope he doesn't end up marrying her. Really don't fancy Barbara as my wicked stepmother.'

'Oh, I don't suppose he'll marry her. Dad and I haven't had this conversation ourselves yet. He doesn't know about my man, in case you speak to him. I'm not even going to tell Tilly – I don't want things to be awkward for her when she sees Dad in the village . . .'

'Don't worry – I won't say a word. So is it serious? With this guy?'

'Very much so in terms of feelings but there's a complication. He has less than a year to live. He has a brain tumour.'

'Shit!' Luke replied, clearly shocked. 'Mum, you sure know how to pick 'em!'

Despite everything, Summer smiled. 'Will you tell Levi? He might be a bit worried about it all – you know what he's like. Tell him to give me a call.'

'I will. Listen, Mum, I'm sorry this new man of yours hasn't got long left, but you'll make the most of it, won't you? Enjoy your time with him?'

Summer smiled again. 'I will, my darling. Thank you for being so understanding. Speak again soon.'

Summer hung up, feeling supremely grateful at having such a mature and empathetic son. Then she looked at the phone again. *I wonder* . . . It was always a gamble calling her parents, as they spent a lot of time in areas where there was no mobile reception, but it was worth a try. The phone rang. It sounded like a European dialling tone.

'*Oui, allo!*' came the voice at the other end.

'Vita, it's me, Summer!'

'No way! It isn't you, is it? You sound so close by!'

'Well, where are you?'

'Brittany, a tiny village near a place called St Malo. I'm sorry we haven't been in touch for such an age, but my phone ran out of battery. I lost my charger. Frank said he had it *somewhere* but he didn't so then I had to buy a new one. There are never any payphones anywhere nowadays . . . Anyway, enough excuses. You know I think about you every day. You feel it, don't you?' she asked, sounding suddenly worried.

'Of course, Vita. Don't worry – I feel it. But listen, we're nearer to each other than you think. I'm at Sylvie's in Jersey!'

'You're not! How hilarious! We can probably see each other. Look – I'm waving! Can you see me?'

Vita was so daft sometimes, despite her intellect, it was hard to know if she was being serious. Summer laughed. 'How's Frank?' she asked.

'Total opiate addict now,' Vita whispered. 'But he's in denial, which is why I'm whispering, because he's only standing a foot away from me.'

Summer heard her father protest. 'I am *not* an addict. Never have been, never will be!' He came on the line. 'Summer, my gorgeous girl, you know she's telling lies, right? I *am* on a bit of medication for my dodgy knee, but that's all . . .'

'Sure, Frank. How is the knee?'

'Better when I take the drugs,' he laughed, and Summer couldn't help smiling. She'd long ago come to terms with her father's penchant for drugs, though it had been frustrating at times when she'd been growing up. She knew her relationship with her father had played some part in the attraction she'd felt towards Seth, who'd offered a sense of stability that she'd never known before. She hadn't realised back then the trade-off she'd end up having to make for such security.

'Hand me back to Vita!' she ordered jokingly. Her mother came back on the line. 'Listen, seeing as you're so near, why don't you come and stay? I've got this man,' she said, knowing her parents would take this news in their stride, 'but there's another bedroom you and Frank could use.'

'A man? What, Seth or a different one?'

'A different one. I'll explain it all when you're here. Will you come?'

'Love to!' agreed Vita. 'We're doing this meditation retreat for the next couple of weeks but we could pop over after that? Catch the boat type thing?'

'The ferry . . . Perfect! Just let me know when you're on your way.'

'Will do, darling! See you soon! Love you heaps! *Ciao, ciao!*'

'Bye, Vita!'

Summer put the phone down and smiled. Then picked it up again when she heard it bleep.

Meet me at the lighthouse? the text said. It was from Jude. He must have changed his flight and returned a day early! She felt giddy with excitement.

Too right! she replied, and she found her flip-flops and hurried along the road towards Corbière. It was a mild evening and there was no traffic, so as she scurried along all she could hear was birdsong. She arrived at the car park and spotted Jude's car, but he wasn't in it. She knew where he'd be and fortunately the tide was far out this time. She made her way down past the bunkers and towards the pathway that led to the lighthouse. There was no one else there, just a solitary figure sitting on a bench watching the sun setting. By the time she reached him, the sun was about to dip out of sight.

'You just made it!' smiled Jude as he pulled Summer towards him and kissed her. 'Look, it's about to vanish! I was just wondering what the lighthouse is like in winter.'

Summer laughed. 'Pretty much the same, I'd have thought! Why in winter?'

'My favourite season.'

'That figures,' Summer said, smiling. 'I'd have guessed as much. I'm definitely a summer person.'

'The most perfectly named person. And, look, just like that it's gone. The sun.'

Jude turned to Summer and kissed her properly.

'I missed you!' said Summer at last. 'I missed you too much.'

'Me too, though the trip was worthwhile. I'll tell you all about it, but shall we go for a walk along the beach now? I need to stretch my legs after the travelling.'

'Sure,' Summer agreed, and they walked back towards Mandla and straight down to the beach. Here, the sky was reflected in the shoreline and the sand gleamed an iridescent pink. It was almost magical in its beauty.

'So what's happening about your parents?' she asked.

'They're coming over in a couple of weeks' time. I've suggested they rent one of those new apartments along the road.'

'It'll be wonderful to meet them. And funnily enough I spoke to my parents earlier and they're going to visit in a couple of weeks too. I offered for them to stay with us – is that okay?'

'Fine with me. I'm sure it'll be an eye-opener! A couple of old hippies in the cottage with us. Looks like we'd better make the most of our next two weeks before we're descended on by family.'

'We're only a little way through your bucket list, too! We'd better get on with it. Let's head home and call up the hotel now. See if they have a room for tomorrow night.'

Chapter Twenty-Three

JUDE'S BUCKET LIST:

4. STAY AT A FIVE-STAR HOTEL

'I can't believe you've never been in love before,' said Summer as she stirred her mojito. They were sitting on the hotel terrace, beside the pool, watching the sun set over the five-mile beach below. Summer had, probably for the first time since meeting Jude, made a proper effort with her make-up and outfit, going for her 60s vibe with an eye-flick and pink lip gloss and wearing a simple black-and-white gingham mini-dress with a Peter Pan collar.

'It's true,' smiled Jude, tucking into some peanuts in the dish beside him. He too looked spruce, in a Superdry shirt and smart black jeans, deeply tanned now and smelling of his lemony cologne.

'But you must have had girlfriends. You definitely don't seem like a novice in the bedroom,' she whispered.

Jude laughed. 'Of course I've had girlfriends. My first one – Olivia – I was definitely in lust with. But we were both too young for love. Then there was Dominique – she was French and very intense and passionate. Again, the passion was there for me, but not the love. Too many arguments. After that, I had a string of hopeless affairs that didn't amount to anything, especially after the incident at school. Then there was Miranda, a couple of years ago. We had a very comfortable relationship. Very cosy and undemanding. She even moved in with me for a bit. But it wasn't based on lust or love. It was based on a mutual passion for Indian takeaways and an addiction to *Dexter* and reruns of *Friends*. I started to think I'd never fall in love or maybe I had but hadn't noticed. Now, of course, I know what it's like . . .'

'Pretty amazing!' Summer agreed. 'Talking of *Friends*, do you remember the saga about the break? Between Ross and Rachel?'

'Ha! Of course I remember it. Did you talk to your husband about whether either of you could see anyone else? You know, while you're on your break?'

'No! Goodness, no! I mean, I just went along with all his plans . . . My main thought was how nice it would be to enjoy a bit of solitude. I saw it completely as a break – with no doubt about us being together again at the end of it. But then Tilly told me he's having an affair with this woman in the village called Barbara, so goodness knows where that leaves us . . . And now, I . . . I don't know . . . I mean, I'd stay here with you if I could . . . If it were possible.' Summer looked stricken. Jude knew what she was saying. If he were going to live.

'I just wish there wasn't this awful ticking clock on our relationship. Why couldn't we have met a decade ago?' Jude said, taking her hand.

'If only!' Summer agreed, bringing his hand to her lips and kissing it.

'This is too deep,' Jude said, taking a breath. 'We need to lighten up or I'm going to start crying into our supper. Come on, let's make more plans. What's next on the bucket list?'

They instantly began to discuss the next item on the agenda, but during dinner Summer had them on to heavier subjects again.

'Tell me about your life before the diagnosis. Before we met,' she said as she tucked into her scallops. The food was delicious, though perhaps a little fancy for Jude's taste. He wolfed down his starter then sat back and ran a hand through his hair, thinking about his life 'BS', as he thought of it – Before Summer.

'I was pretty down in the dumps. I didn't even realise it at the time, but looking back I can recognise how low I was. I'm naturally cynical, but it was more than that. I hated my job, so there was no joy there. I'd split up with Miranda and my love life was dire. I felt tired, headachy. Well, we know the reason for that now. I wondered if I was depressed, but now I know it was the tumour causing the lethargy.'

Summer eyed him from across the table. She took a sip of her wine. 'Perhaps you were depressed as well. When did you stop dancing?' she asked.

Jude burst out laughing. 'Dancing? What are you talking about?'

'When I was fifteen we lived in Arizona. It was wonderful. Always sunny. A surreal landscape. We were part of a commune – the oldest one in America. It was incredible – a kind of utopia. They were heavily into shamanism so I learnt a lot about all that stuff. My parents were really involved, but I didn't buy into it wholesale. Some of it really resonated, though. Like, if you went to see a medicine man or woman complaining of depression, they'd ask you: when did you stop dancing, singing, being enchanted by stories and enjoying silence? Doesn't that just cut through everything? A healthy soul *needs* those things.'

Despite his natural cynicism, Jude smiled. 'You had such an interesting upbringing. No wonder you're so fascinating. Arizona. There was this song out when I was a kid – "Little Fluffy Clouds". I remember the girl in the song went on about the sunsets in the desert.'

'They have to be seen to be believed. You know, until I met you, I don't think anyone I've ever met has seen my childhood as interesting in a positive way. They've always been intrigued but horrified as well. One of the things I love about you is that you get it. You see how incredible it was for me. But you never answered my question. When did you stop dancing?'

'Summer, in truth, I never started.'

'Come on! Surely as a child you must have enjoyed a boogie? Or at least as a teenager?'

'No – seriously! I've always just found it deeply embarrassing!'

'Then it's time you gave it a try!'

Chapter Twenty-Four

JUDE'S BUCKET LIST:

5. NEW IN AT NUMBER 5 – GO DANCING!

Summer woke up with her ears ringing. She couldn't actually remember the last time that had happened. She smiled as she thought back to the night before. There they'd been, staying in a highly civilised hotel far out west, and after an exquisite three-course meal, Summer had dragged Jude into town to go dancing.

'Where shall we go?' she'd asked, alive with excitement at doing something that seemed – at the age of thirty-eight – rather wild. The taxi dropped them off in Bath Street and Jude scratched his head, trying to think where they might try.

'There's a place down here, I think,' he said, leading Summer past groups of screeching girls and overly loud men – all completely plastered. 'I think they got in trouble for refusing to let older ladies in or something. It made the news at the time – my friend's girlfriend covered the story. She's a journalist like you.'

'Hand, please,' the bouncer said as they reached the entrance.

'Why?' asked Summer.

'Stamp,' the steroid-pumped bouncer replied, looking at her with dead eyes.

'What for?'

'So you can get back in if you come outside for a fag or whatever. You gonna be a trouble-maker?'

'No, no,' Summer replied, compliantly proffering her hand. Finally, they were in. It wasn't that Summer had never been clubbing – of course she had – but it was perfectly possible she hadn't been to a club in the last decade and she soon realised her hearing had deteriorated in that time. She literally couldn't hear a word Jude said to her, even when he was shouting in her ear. They took to conducting themselves like they were deaf and dumb, signing if either needed to use the loos or to offer another drink. After a couple of confidence-boosting shots, Summer performed a little shimmy to suggest they dance. She wanted to seize the opportunity while it was a tune she recognised – up until then the music had just been hideous noise.

'Come on!' she shouted, and Jude reluctantly followed her. Soon, though, he was into the swing of it – any embarrassment clearly completely forgotten – and they busted some moves, overcome by a kind of reckless euphoria taken for granted by all the kids who were bouncing around beside them. Before long they were sweaty and thirsty, but they didn't want to break the spell and fortunately the DJ kept on coming up with the goods, playing music they knew. Music that was conducive to throwing up their arms and swinging their hips. They danced non-stop for an hour and a half. After that, they left, but they couldn't find a taxi for love nor money.

'At least we won't have to sleep on the streets. We can head to my flat. I've got the keys on me,' said Jude.

'Guess our night of luxury at the Atlantic is going to be wasted then. Those sheets looked dreamy, too. Egyptian cotton.'

'How do you know you won't get better at mine?' Jude laughed. 'Actually, don't get your hopes up. It's pretty crap.'

'But it's yours and I'm dying to see it, even if we are failing at number four on the list. We'll have to try again another night.'

They'd reached Jude's block of flats and wobbled down several steps to his basement doorstep. 'It doesn't matter. I've got a feel for what it's like to stay in a five-star place now. Very nice, but actually I couldn't really care less where I am as long as I'm with you.' Jude looked up, startled, as if he couldn't believe those words had come out of his mouth. Summer kissed him, then waited as he fumbled around with his keys.

'This is it,' Jude said a moment later, turning on the hall light and blushing deeply. 'I've just realised what a stark contrast it is to the Atlantic Hotel and Mandla. It's like I'm seeing the place with fresh eyes. It's how I always feel when I'm buying new trainers and I suddenly notice how scruffy the old ones seem. I feel mortified I've been seen wearing them in public for months on end.'

'Jude, I've only seen the hallway so far. Come on, give me a tour.'

'All right,' sighed Jude, switching on more lights. 'This is the sitting room . . . And the kitchen. That's the bathroom,' he said, pointing at the door, 'and this is my room,' he finished. It was a whistle-stop tour and Summer felt slightly out of breath. She sat down on the badly made bed.

'I love it!'

'You do?' Jude looked incredulous. 'But it's so scruffy and stark and crappy. You live in this amazing, luxuriously decorated place . . .'

'But it's not mine, remember? I mean, I love Mandla too – who wouldn't? But my house in England isn't like that. It's a bit tidier than this, but I don't have a flair for interior design any more than you do. What I love about this place is that it's *you*. No frills. It's honest. If I lived alone, or with you, this is how it would be. A place to be. Right now, a place to be together.'

'I love you, Summer,' Jude said, sitting down next to her on the bed.

'Jude, I love you too.' Summer looked like she might cry but instead she kissed him and they began to take each other's clothes off. The bed was squeaky and after a while there was a banging sound on the ceiling. Clearly the neighbours above weren't amused.

'Should we stop?' giggled Summer.

'No,' said Jude. 'The bastards have been keeping me awake for years. Let's not stop for a moment.'

And they didn't.

Chapter Twenty-Five

JUDE'S BUCKET LIST:

6. GET A RESCUE DOG

'Shall we go somewhere for breakfast?' suggested Summer, after rooting around in the kitchen cupboards. Jude was embarrassed that he had little to offer other than stale cornflakes.

'Good plan. I'll take you to my favourite café in the market.'

'It'll be lovely to see more of St Helier. I only popped in briefly on my first day to pick up some clothes after some idiot nicked my suitcase at the airport.'

'No way! That happened to me, too. A total muppet stole my case at the start of the summer. I had to make a TV appeal to get it back!'

'Ha ha! It wasn't just a straightforward suitcase swap in the end, was it?' marvelled Summer. She checked her watch. 'Nine o'clock. Shall we head in now, then?'

'Yep, I'll just grab my post, then we can go.'

Five minutes later they were walking through the back streets into town. When they reached the central market, Summer was awestruck.

'Oh, it's beautiful!' she said, taking in the vast stone building with its glass roof and red gates. Jude saw it as if with fresh eyes and realised how attractive the place was. 'And so old-fashioned. I hope everyone uses it? It would be a shame if the stalls couldn't keep going.'

'I've always used it myself, but a lot of people don't – they want the convenience of a massive supermarket and easy parking. You should see it in here at Christmastime. It's so festive, with all the trees and mistletoe. You'd love it.'

Summer was like a kid in a sweetshop. She positively bounced around the place. 'It's amazing! Look at all the florists and fruit and veg stalls. What else? A butcher's, a bakery. A deli. Is that a haberdashery? You're kidding me! I can just imagine elderly ladies pulling their tartan trollies around the market, buying their groceries and their knitting wool all under one roof. And look at this shop, it's like something out of the fifties!'

Summer's eyes were darting about as she took in the enormous array of goods on offer at Red Triangle Stores – it seemed to sell everything you could possibly need, from children's toys to plant pots to ornamental gifts and even suitcases.

'You should buy one of these,' Summer said, pointing to a particularly garish case. 'It'll stop people running off with your grey one!'

'I'm rather fond of the grey one, I'll have you know, though it's served its purpose. I'm not interested in meeting any more suitcase thieves. Just along there, look, that's the café – Bisson's, it's called. Just past the fountain and along a bit.'

'Why do you go to the drabbest-looking one? There's loads that look much nicer! The food must be good!'

'It is!' Jude said, and he ushered Summer along and tried not to laugh when Mrs Bisson arrived at the table with a grimly set jaw and virtually threw the menus at them with a sigh.

'I'll have the cooked breakfast, please, and a white coffee,' Jude said five minutes later when Mrs Bisson returned to take their order. This harmless request prompted another large sigh. Summer looked up in surprise and caught Jude's eye. He suddenly felt quite hysterical and had to start coughing to mask his laughter. Summer was clearly feeling the same – when she placed her order her voice sounded strangled, which only added to Jude's mirth.

'Scrambled egg on granary toast and an orange juice,' Summer managed and, with a further sigh that almost tipped them over the edge, Mrs Bisson grabbed the menus back and plodded off to the kitchen. Jude and Summer both let out a wail of laughter and Summer began dabbing at her streaming eyes.

'Sssh!' Jude said in the end, flapping his hands in front of his face to try to stop himself laughing. 'She'll be back in a sec! We'll probably get detention if she catches us laughing!'

They both managed to make a monumental effort to keep their faces straight and Summer pulled the *Telegraph* out of her bag so they could distract themselves with the cryptic crossword. They'd only recently discovered how much both of them enjoyed this daily challenge and it was so much more enjoyable – and successful – doing it together.

'This one's an anagram of "voices rant on", I think,' Jude said, pointing at one across. 'You're good at those . . .'

'Conversation.'

'Very quick!' Jude said, impressed.

The next thing they knew, Mrs Bisson was back. 'Tsch! Move that newspaper . . . How can I serve with that in the way?' she growled.

'Sorry,' Jude meekly apologised, lowering the newspaper to his lap.

'One fry-up?' she asked, though she'd only taken their order fifteen minutes before and Jude couldn't believe she was unable to remember who'd ordered what.

'That's me, thanks,' said Jude.

'One scrambled eggs?' she asked next, and Jude's hysteria was close to resurfacing. It was incredibly tempting to tell her that it must be for the old man on the table opposite.

'That'll be for me,' Summer said with a smile.

Once the old battleaxe had disappeared, they tucked in.

'How is it?' Summer asked as she watched Jude delve into the greasy sausages and bacon.

'Erm . . . Actually, this is strange . . . You know, it doesn't taste quite as good as I remember!'

'I've converted you to healthy eating, haven't I? Jude, my scrambled eggs are pretty hideous too – all sloppy. Let's just pay and leave . . . I spotted somewhere far nicer.'

'But if I don't eat up she'll have my guts for garters!'

'She's in the kitchen, and you're not going to come back here now anyway, are you? Come on, I'll leave some cash, then let's get going!'

'No, no. I'm paying,' Jude said, peeling out some notes and leaving them on the table.

They ran from the place, the old man looking on in amusement, fortunately making it out before the terrifying Mrs Bisson reappeared.

'Follow me!' said Summer, and Jude scurried to keep up with her as she headed towards the Italian deli.

'Two bruschettas, please!' Summer asked the man behind the counter. She paid and they made their way to a bench, where they sat and ate them out of paper bags. Lightly toasted French bread sprinkled with quality Italian olive oil and topped with diced fresh tomatoes, a sprig of basil and some ground pepper.

'These are fantastic,' Jude said. 'A miles-better choice. Summer, I wish I'd met you years ago. It's like I've been blindfolded all my life and now you've come along and I can see at last.'

For the rest of the day, Jude noticed the subtle magical effect Summer had on him. They wandered along the streets and he found himself observing so many things he'd never even spotted before.

'Check that out!' Summer laughed as they walked towards Charing Cross. 'Up there! A denture repair centre! How cool is that!' Jude looked up and saw the neon sign. He tried to calculate how many times he'd walked along this particular street without even looking above eye level.

After their stroll through town, they headed back to Jude's to collect his car (Eddie had borrowed it the day before and returned it to the flat rather than Petit Port – fortunately, it now turned out) and make the return journey to the hotel to collect their bags and then to Mandla. On the way back, Summer spotted a signpost.

'Jude, look – the animal shelter's up that lane. Why don't we turn back and see if they've got a rescue dog? That's on your list, isn't it?'

Jude pulled over. 'Well, it is, but I didn't think I'd really achieve that one. It's not fair on the poor animal, is it? I mean, if I'm not going to be around for much longer . . .'

'But there'll be two of us getting the dog,' Summer said gently. 'I promise – I'll take care of it, if we find one. I know Sylvie won't mind – she's a huge animal lover, always taking in strays wherever she is in the world.'

'Summer, that would be amazing! I've always wanted a pet but my parents thought they'd be too much of a tie and it didn't seem fair when I was working full-time.'

'And I've always wanted one, too, but Seth's allergic.'

'But what if you go back to him . . .'

'Jude, I'm not going back to him. I was thinking about it, after you asked last night. The fact is, I've fallen completely in love with you and entirely out of love with him. I couldn't go back now . . .'

Jude couldn't believe his luck and yet his bad luck, too. How bittersweet it all was. 'Are you going to tell him?'

'Not now. I know it's bad, but there's scope for it to all get horribly dramatic. I mean, given that he's now with Barbara, it would probably all be fine, but I don't want to risk telling him for the moment. He might end up coming over here or something. I don't want anything to interfere with our time together, not for now. When the six months is up, whatever your situation is, I'll head back and tell him we're finished, then I'll come straight over here again. For the moment, though, I'm going to let sleeping dogs lie.'

Jude smiled, feeling immense relief. She'd picked him, after all, and, even if there couldn't be a long future for them, he was glad he knew she'd chosen him over Seth. 'Well, talking of sleeping dogs,' he said, and he swung the car back so they could take the lane up towards the shelter.

An hour later they were back in the car with their new charge, having fallen instantly in love with a black Labrador called Prinny.

'Prince, actually, but we call him Prinny,' the lady had told them. 'He was born on the twenty-second of July 2013 – the same day as Prince George, hence the name. He's young, but sadly he has a condition that makes him seem much older. He's got quite a short life expectancy, I'm afraid, which is why nobody's been interested in giving him a home. They don't want to get attached, only to lose him.'

Jude saw that Summer's eyes had filled with tears. 'Poor boy, we're in the same boat,' Jude told the dog, stroking his silky fur. He had enormous, soft brown eyes and instantly proffered a paw first to Jude and then to Summer. That was it – they simply had to have him.

'I can't believe I've fallen in love with two men who are going to leave me,' Summer said sadly as they arrived back at Mandla and settled Prinny into his new home.

'But not yet,' Jude said, pulling her into a hug to hide the emotion he knew must be written all over his face. 'Not yet.'

Chapter Twenty-Six

JUDE'S BUCKET LIST:

7. TAKE BALLET LESSONS

They were comfortable enough with each other now to take their lenses out in the early evening and wear their glasses instead, a relief as the constant sunshine seemed to make their eyes more tired than usual. They were ensconced on the sofa one evening watching *Great Canal Journeys*.

'How long have you worn specs for?' Jude asked, passing a bowl of popcorn to Summer. She was sitting at right angles to him, her tanned feet in his lap, while Prinny lay on the hearthrug.

'Since I was a teenager. How about you?'

'I was younger – about seven or eight.'

'Did it bother you?'

'Not at first, but I did get teased a bit at secondary school and it was tricky with my sport, so I got contacts when I was about fourteen.'

'I only started wearing lenses when we moved back from Arizona when I was sixteen. For me, it was down to the fact that I kept losing my glasses! I always was a scatterbrain. Luckily I was never teased about it, but then I never went to school. I can never understand why kids get a tough time for wearing glasses.'

'I guess those of us who wear them tend to feel a little bit different and low in confidence, so we're prime targets. And kids – older ones, anyway – always seem to feel threatened by anyone who's a bit different, like it's a threat to them in some inexplicable way. But wearing glasses wasn't the worst thing I was teased for . . .'

'No? What was then?' asked Summer, turning down the volume on the TV.

'When I was about thirteen I was probably at my most dorky, although I was playing rugby so I wasn't considered a *complete* nerd. Anyway, one day we had a ballet company come to the school to perform. Most of my mates laughed the whole way through it, distracted by the men's packages in the white tights, but I was mesmerised. I was blown away, not just by the beauty of it, but by the strength.

'The following week a teacher from the nearby girls' school said she was going to start ballet classes on a Tuesday evening and she was looking for male and female students. There was this sign up about it and I took note of the time of the first class and didn't mention it to anyone. When the day arrived I was so nervous, but I went along. I wasn't really expecting any other boys to be there, and there weren't. The teacher was thrilled I'd turned up and most of the girls were sweet and friendly. But one girl – Julie, she was called . . . She kept whispering behind her hand with one of her friends and laughing at me as I tried my best to master a plié.

'I should have known my secret would never be kept and, of course, Julie went straight home and told her brother, who was a fantastic rugby player – in the firsts at my school. He was also a complete sadist. The day after my ballet class I had my head shoved down the loo, my lunch nicked and basically my self-esteem squashed into the ground. I was called Fairy Boy for at least a year, when thankfully Julie's brother was expelled and I began to blend into the background once again.'

'Poor boy – I could cry! So what happened with the lessons then? Did you ever go again?'

'Of course not!'

'Are they on your bucket list?' asked Summer, and Jude was quiet, then smiled. 'They are, aren't they?'

'Yep, although – a bit like getting a rescue dog – I didn't really think I'd actually go . . . I wouldn't know where to find a class, for one thing.'

'I think I might know, actually . . .'

'What? But you're not even local!'

'I know, but when we were at the Co-op yesterday I saw a notice about adult lessons at the parish hall in St Ouen's. A lady called Madame Vivier runs them. I guess it jumped out at me, as I've always wanted to try ballet too. My upbringing was way too freestyle for anything so disciplined. Shall we see if we can join the class together?'

'Why not?' Jude grinned. 'It'll be fun. But don't you dare laugh at me in my white tights!'

'Ha ha, you're not wearing white tights on my watch, thank you very much. Some jogging bottoms will do you nicely. Now let's get another drink.'

As it turned out, they enjoyed quite a few more drinks and the next morning they felt lazy, so decided to idle in bed after Prinny had been let out for his morning business. He was lying at the end of the bed, snoring gently, while Jude and Summer tried to finish the previous day's crossword. They were just pondering the final clue when there was a knock at the door. They both jumped, entirely unused to any callers, though Prinny didn't stir.

'I'd better go,' said Summer, and she wrapped her dressing gown round her and went to the door.

'Very good morning to you, my dear!' the man at the door chirped. Summer didn't have a clue who he was but she recognised him immediately as someone who might be described as 'larger than life'. 'Dennis Gallichan!' the man said, introducing himself. 'Own the new holiday apartments just along the road. Great buddies with Sylvie. She's always awfully generous with the whisky bottle, ho ho!'

'Ah, Dennis – yes, she's mentioned you! Would you like to come in? I don't have any whisky but you're welcome to have a coffee!'

'Ha ha! Even I don't touch a drop till it's midday in France, bah ha! A coffee would be most kind, thank you, my dear. Just thought I'd pop in and say hi-de-hi. Been meaning to all summer but it's been a busy old time of late, what with the problems with Mimsy.'

Summer realised Dennis was one of those people who dropped their friends' names into conversation as if you knew them. 'Mimsy?' she asked, popping the kettle on.

'Yes, my dear old Lab. She got run over by one of those heinous boy racers that charge up and down these lanes out west – "hoons", my Aussie pal would call them. It was touch and go for a while but she's pulled through, thank goodness. Can't imagine life without my dear Mims.'

'I'm glad she's okay. We've got a Lab, too,' Summer said, and at that moment Prinny hobbled through, with Jude trailing after him carrying the paper. He discarded it on the table.

'Squire! Very nice to meet you!' Dennis said to Jude, heaving his rotund figure up from the chair he'd just seated himself on to shake Jude's hand. He then crouched down, with considerable effort. 'And jolly pleased to meet you too, dear fellow,' he said, giving Prinny a good rub.

'This is Dennis, a friend of Sylvie's,' Summer explained to Jude. 'This is my boyfriend, Jude,' she added, turning back to Dennis and handing him his coffee. She realised it was the first time she'd introduced

Jude as her boyfriend. It felt like such an immature word, but 'lover' seemed a bit racy and 'partner' too formal.

'Now, let me work this out,' said Dennis, taking a sip of his drink. 'You're the niece who's staying here for a few months. Hmmm, husband trouble, Sylvie said . . . Is it all over then, now?'

'Yes, it sort of is,' Summer replied. Then, keen to move the conversation on, she began to ask Dennis all about himself and the island. He was clearly a proud islander and was more than happy to hold forth about the beauty and history of the place – in quite some detail. Summer spotted Jude's eyes starting to glaze over and decided that, if she didn't take some action, Dennis would be ready for his first drink of the day.

'It's all so interesting,' Summer told him. 'But we really ought to take Prinny for a walk in a minute. He'll be getting restless soon.'

Dennis looked at Prinny, who looked anything but restless as he lay dozily in his bed. But, to his credit, he took his cue. 'Right-o, best be off – get home to check on Mimsy. Wife died at Christmas. Not so good at fending for myself. Going to be slipping down the plughole soon if I lose any more weight!' he chortled, standing up and rubbing his vast tummy.

Summer couldn't help herself – she felt sorry for him. It was clear that underneath the cheeriness he was lonely without his wife. 'Come and join us for supper one night,' she said, and she felt Jude shoot her a glance. 'Let me have your number and we'll get something organised.'

'Too kind, too kind!' Dennis replied, and he proffered a business card slipped from his shirt breast pocket. 'Most obliged! Toodle-pip!'

He left, popping his head back round the door a moment later. 'Inedible, by the way!' Jude and Summer looked at him, confused. 'The last clue! The crossword! Bah ha ha!'

He was gone. Jude bundled Summer into a cuddle. '*You* are too soft-hearted!' he admonished.

'But he's sweet really. I know, a bit of a bore, but he's a dog lover at least! And he's good at the crossword. That clue was really bugging me!'

'True enough. We'd better get some decent booze in. He looks like a real bon viveur to me.'

'There you go!' Summer smiled. 'I'm not the only soft-hearted one around here! Now, we'd better get dressed and take our restless hound for a walk.'

Prinny jumped up, in Pavlovian fashion, at the word 'walk', then yawned loudly and took himself back to bed.

Chapter Twenty-Seven

Jude's bucket list:

8. A post-coital cigarette

The day after the visit from Dennis had been another bad one for Jude – the worst yet. It had knocked him for six for forty-eight hours. But it was now a few days later and he felt much better again. It was about nine in the morning and he was enjoying, or perhaps a better word was 'experiencing', his first ever post-coital cigarette.

'How is it?' asked Summer. She'd never been a smoker but wasn't averse to the smell of cigarette smoke so she was quite happy to relax in the bed next to Jude while he puffed away. Seth would never have contemplated having a cigarette, being dreadfully asthmatic, so she hadn't been a passive smoker for a long time – not since she was a kid, when her dad had smoked his roll-ups around her.

Jude coughed. 'Actually, it's disgusting!' he admitted, quite pleased that he wasn't going to start up a twenty-a-day habit for the last months of his life. 'Let me get rid of it and clean my teeth.' Summer laughed and Jude pottered off to the kitchen to dispose of the offending fag then fuss Prinny, who was happily ensconced in his bed. Jude had already let him out earlier in the morning. Then he padded along to the bathroom to clean his teeth. He was just rinsing his toothbrush when he heard Summer talking to someone. Strange. He went back through to the bedroom.

'Here he is now,' said Summer, and she passed over the phone. She looked a bit funny.

'Thanks,' said Jude and, without thinking, he returned to the bathroom with the handset. The phone so rarely rang for him (unlike Summer, who often spoke to her boys or occasionally her friend Tilly), he wasn't sure where to take the call. After five minutes, he re-emerged. Summer was quiet.

'Please don't think I'm an eavesdropper,' she said eventually, 'but the acoustics in the bathroom made your voice echo. Who is she? Cat?'

'Are you jealous?' Jude teased, realising the cause of Summer's unusually subdued countenance.

Summer looked startled. 'Do you know, I think I might be! I've never felt jealous before . . . Do I have reason to be? She sounded very sexy. And I heard you arrange to meet her tonight.'

'Not just me – you as well. And you've no reason to worry,' Jude smiled. 'She's just my friend Eddie's girlfriend. She's the one who's a journalist – I've told you about her. She was really supportive when I first got the news about the brain tumour. They've been away visiting her family in Portugal, but they're back now and she wants to meet you. Would you mind getting together with them tonight?'

'Not at all,' Summer replied, looking relieved. 'I'm sorry about that. What a horrible green-eyed monster!'

'You're not the only one. Every time I think about Seth I feel sick. Tell me about him.'

'What do you want to know?'

'Well, for starters, what does he look like?'

'Tall, dark and handsome.' Jude looked aghast and Summer giggled. 'But also quite *frowny*. He's such a serious person – solemn. Always looking a bit cross, though he doesn't verbally complain all that much. He has a temper, though. He doesn't shout or anything, but he gets physically violent. Not with me or the boys,' Summer quickly added, seeing Jude's face. 'But he'll suddenly make this strange noise and throw a plate across the room. Generally, though, he's very quiet. Non-communicative really.'

'You're not painting a very nice picture!'

'I'm not, am I? But that's because I'm still hurt that he packed me off for six months and is now having it off with Barbara Robinson! Mind you, I've cause to be very grateful to him for that now. Anyway, he does have his good points.'

'Such as?'

'Well, he's not unkind. As I say, he gets into a filthy temper every so often, which isn't pleasant, but in fairness it's usually his mother that provokes him into plate-throwing and half the time I'm tempted to join him. And he's very talented musically – a brilliant pianist. My friend Tilly is a violinist so they at least have that in common. Otherwise they fight like cat and dog. It's exhausting. Have you ever had that? Where a friend and lover don't hit it off?'

'Yep! I thought Miranda was incredibly easy-going and nearly everyone who met her liked her. But Eddie couldn't stand her. Nor could Cat. I never could work out why.'

'Oh, great! What are they going to think of me? What if they hate me too? Now I'm nervous about tonight!'

'They'll love you!' Jude said confidently. 'Honestly, you don't need to worry.'

It turned out they really did. Cat and Summer got on like a house on fire, instantly chatting about their work and the joys and trials of having children while they waited for the pub to serve their supper and the boys discussed football, though Jude was half-listening to the girls, interested in getting a picture of Summer as a mother.

'It's the sleeping-in I miss,' Cat complained. 'They're up at six every bloody morning – sometimes even earlier at weekends.'

'I remember those years, but it gets better – I promise. They do start sleeping in eventually,' Summer comforted. 'The only problem is that it usually coincides with them turning into recluses who barely venture out of their rooms. It's like that with kids, isn't it? One problem solved and, hey presto, a different one appears!'

'It's the hardest job and nothing prepares you, does it? Mind you, my sister's struggling to get pregnant at the moment and she'd give her right arm for a couple of kids, so she's always on at me about how grateful I should be.'

'That's a pressure in itself, isn't it? Everyone you talk to in those early years says, *Enjoy them while they're young. They grow up too soon!* and I remember thinking, *But you're not the one being kept up half the night and trying to catch sick in a bucket when they've caught yet another bug!* Though it *is* true, what those irritating people tell you – they are the best years in so many ways.'

'Did you work when your kids were small?' Cat asked.

'Oh yes, I was only eighteen when I had them and my husband was training to be a teacher. We needed some income. I was a barmaid for a while but I'd always loved writing, so when a position came up at the local paper I applied for it. I've no idea how, but I got it. It was really tough, trying to make it fit in with the children, and during school holidays the childcare costs weren't far off what I was earning. But I liked the feeling of independence it gave me – earning my own money and doing something I loved. I thought it was probably a good example to set the boys, too, although I was always feeling guilty – like I couldn't give my all to anyone.'

'Yeah, I know that feeling. I want to know more about the kind of journalism you do but I'm dying for a pee. I'll be back in a sec,' Cat said, grabbing her bag.

'I'll get some more drinks in. What would you like?'

'Vodka and coke again, thanks,' Cat replied, heading towards the corridor that signed to the ladies.

Jude and Eddie placed their order with Summer, too, and while Eddie started chatting to a work colleague he'd bumped into, Jude took the opportunity to head to the loo himself. He followed the sign towards the corridor, turned the corner and stopped dead still. Cat was talking on her phone in Portuguese surrounded by three men with skinheads, who were blocking her way to the ladies. Jude saw her hastily put the phone in her bag.

'You here to clean the toilets?' one of them asked her. 'That's all you porko Portuguese are good for, isn't it?' he sneered.

Jude was expecting Cat to shoot them down in flames with one of her usual blunt and feisty ripostes but she just stood there, looking petrified, completely silent. Jude saw red.

'What the hell are you arseholes doing?' he shouted, storming towards them.

'Oh, hey up! It's the knight in shining armour! She clean your toilets, too, does she? Bet that's not all she does.'

That was it. Jude swung for the ringleader, socking him on the nose, which immediately began to spurt blood in a cartoonish fashion.

'What the . . . ?' the man replied, his hand dabbing at his bloody face. 'I think you've broken my nose, you cock!'

Jude braced himself for a proper fight. It was only him against the three of them and he felt a moment of trepidation, thinking back to that devastating evening when Melvin had stabbed him in the stomach, but then, unexpectedly, the men shot off, cursing as they ran towards the door, determined to have the last word.

'I'm on probation – otherwise I'd be finishing you! I could have you!' the ringleader shouted at Jude as he made his exit.

'Ow!' Jude said, belatedly, his fist feeling sore and bruised. 'Cat, are you okay?'

'Shit, yeah . . . I'm shaken up, but bloody impressed. Jude, I can't believe you put yourself in danger like that for me.'

'Don't be daft,' he said, but as they went to rejoin the others Cat was full of praise for Jude's bravery.

'He was amazing!' she told Eddie and Summer, who were horrified this had all been going on without them even realising it. With the story told, Cat realised she still needed the loo.

'I'm coming with you,' said Eddie. 'I'll guard you!'

With Eddie and Cat out of earshot, Summer asked Jude for details. He was still shaking from the adrenaline rush, but he felt a sense of achievement, too, at how he'd instinctively dealt with the situation.

'What were they doing?' she asked.

'Being threatening. Being racist. That's what really got me. I thought back to Di telling us all about the Nazi occupation. I remember her saying how, to her, it seemed as though the war was essentially one of tolerance versus evil. And then you get tossers like those guys, being so bloody intolerant and racist.'

'There's more of your ancestors in you than you first thought,' Summer smiled. 'Ah, here's our food at last. Jude, I love your friends!'

'I hoped you would. But we mustn't stay too late. I need to be fresh for the final thing on the bucket list tomorrow!'

'I can't believe it's the last one. You don't ask for much, do you?'

'I've no need to. The time I'm spending with you – it's better than the most extravagant bucket list I could have ever come up with.'

'Pass the sick bowl,' Eddie teased as he and Cat rejoined them, bringing Jude and Summer right back down to earth.

Chapter Twenty-Eight

JUDE'S BUCKET LIST:

9. DRIVE A FLASHY CAR

'So you're a TVR enthusiast, then, are you, Mr De Carteret?' the man asked. He had a raspy voice and looked like a sly fox. He had a tiny head, with gingery hair pasted down with gel, and narrow eyes that were unfeasibly close together.

'Well, in theory,' Jude explained. 'I've never been able to afford one. Until now,' he added, no doubt remembering that, in order to test-drive one, he needed to pretend he might actually buy it.

'What are you thinking then? The Griffith, the Tamora?' the fox asked, leading Jude along rows of shining cars. Summer peered inside them. They were immaculate – little fox obviously spent hours polishing all the steering wheels. 'The Cerbera, maybe?' the salesman continued. 'Or . . .' He paused for dramatic effect. 'The Tuscan!' He stopped and presented with a flourish an electric-blue convertible that even Summer, who had no interest in cars, was impressed with.

'It's kind of space-agey,' she remarked, running a hand along the paintwork. Jude was speechless. He looked as if he were mesmerised by its glamour. Eventually, he seemed to get a grip. 'Can we take this one for a test drive?' he asked, clearly trying to sound nonchalant.

Five minutes later they were sitting in comfort on pristine leather seats that gave off an almost erotic scent of wealth and privilege.

'I'm shaking,' Jude said, grinning at Summer. 'I have never in my life even sat in a car like this, let alone driven one.'

'I'll drive, if you like,' Summer teased.

'No way!' Jude laughed, and he switched the engine on. 'Listen to that!' he said next, at the deep roar of the throbbing vehicle – so strong their bodies were vibrating.

'Here we go!' And that was it – they were off. Right out of the garage and, with a few clunky changes of gear, off towards the Avenue, where it seemed as if Jude was struggling to keep the car down to the legal maximum limit for Jersey – forty miles an hour. Moments later, they hit traffic and ground to a halt.

'This would be so frustrating,' Jude said, glancing across at Summer, whose hair was all over the place.

'You'd have to nip across to France all the time to give the car a proper spin, wouldn't you?'

'Yeah, I guess the regular expense of the ferry would be nothing if you owned a car like this. Can you imagine?'

'How does it feel to drive?'

'Incredible!' Jude grinned, though the smile was taken off his face a moment later.

'Wankers!' a group of young lads shouted towards the car from The Burger, at the end of the Avenue.

'What the . . . ?' Jude asked, looking at Summer. 'Why are they calling us wankers?'

Summer laughed. 'It's the car! They think you own it. Jealousy. No one wants someone else's wealth and success flaunted at them so obviously. An electric-blue TVR – it *is* a little attention-seeking!'

It didn't stop there. Every ten minutes or so during their test drive they spotted people flicking the bird at them or shouting abuse for no good reason. A couple of youths even threw chips at them as they drove along the Five Mile Road.

By the time they arrived back at the garage, Jude looked as if he were relieved to be shot of the thing.

'It's been a real lesson,' he said, turning to Summer. 'The car's amazing – but not the baggage that comes with it. I can see now that my parents are on to something with their humble desires in life. Keeping things simple keeps you nicely under the radar.'

Summer laughed. Seth's greatest desire had always been to own a sports car (in his case a Lamborghini) and she was fairly sure he'd have put up with the jealous comments rather than keeping things simple if he'd had the money for one.

'How did it go?' asked Mr Fox, when Jude and Summer emerged from the TVR. 'Would you like to come into my office to discuss payment plans?' He lifted an arm, showing off a large sweat patch staining his blue shirt.

'Actually, I'm going to need to speak to my bank first,' Jude told him, and Summer dug him in the ribs. 'But I loved it! Incredible car!'

'But wait!' the man called as Jude and Summer hotfooted it back to Jude's very mediocre and entirely non-attention-grabbing car. 'My business card!' he called out. 'I haven't even given you my business card!'

Jude began to drive past and, out of sympathy, Summer reached out through the window and took the card.

'Thanks,' she smiled. 'We'll be in touch!' she called back.

'That's what comes of telling fibs and trying to be grand,' Jude said as he settled back into the comfort of his own battered car seat. 'You have to deal with car salesmen and have abuse hurled at you wherever you go!'

'It was fun, though! What shall we do now?'

'I'm just going to pop home and pick up my post, if that's okay. Then we'd better head back and take Prinny for a walk.'

'Jude,' Summer said.

'Yes?'

'You looked seriously sexy driving a TVR.'

Jude turned his head towards Summer and smiled. 'Want to try out my squeaky bed again?' he asked, as he turned into the parking area beside his block of flats. And they did, laughing hysterically when the neighbours above knocked on the ceiling again.

But later the same day, back at Mandla, Summer realised something had changed, the light-hearted mood of earlier in the day usurped by a darker, gloomier feeling.

'Are you okay?' Summer asked Jude, more than once.

'Yep,' he replied each time.

But he wasn't okay. Summer was certain about that.

PART THREE

Falling Apart

Mid-August–November 2017

Chapter Twenty-Nine

JERSEY, AUGUST

SUMMER

The day of the test drive had heralded a disturbing shift in Jude's demeanour that started to cast a shadow over their time together. Summer couldn't work out what had changed.

They were taking Prinny for a walk along the cliffs one morning. Jude was in a particularly sullen, silent kind of mood.

'Jude, come on. Please talk to me. What is it? You haven't been right for days now. You have to talk to me. Maybe I can help?'

Jude remained silent, but eventually he stopped and sat down on a nearby bench. 'It's nearly time . . .' he mumbled.

Summer felt instantly sick. Had his symptoms suddenly worsened? How had she not noticed?

'Time to . . . ?'

'To see the consultant again. Another scan and assessment. Ever since I met you I've tried not to think too much about the reality of it all, but when we drove to the flat the other day to pick up my post I saw I had a letter from the hospital. I read it while you made supper. Summer, I'm so afraid.'

Summer felt an incredible sense of relief. 'You must talk to me, you muppet!' she said. 'Of course you're scared. It's completely natural. When is it?'

'Tomorrow.'

'Then it's nearly done,' she told him and she gripped his hand. 'Let's keep really busy until then. Try not to think about it. Come on, let's head back to Mandla and give Cat and Eddie a call. We could invite them round for dinner?'

Jude smiled – a slightly slow and reluctant one, but a smile nonetheless. 'Okay,' he agreed with a sigh. 'A barbecue? That'll keep me busy.'

'Ideal!' Summer agreed. 'It's the perfect night for it too. I can't believe how amazing the weather's been since that very first day I arrived here.'

'You've got a skewed vision of the place now,' Jude told her as they walked back along the cliffs hand in hand, Prinny gambolling along in front, inadvertently tripping them up every couple of minutes. 'It's not always sunny, you know!'

'Don't believe you!' Summer laughed, but the next day she experienced her first ever taste of what islanders called 'the dreaded fog'.

She woke early and, seeing Jude was finally sleeping after a restless night, she crept out of bed and went through to the kitchen to find Prinny and let him out. The dog was reluctant to move, but eventually hoisted his body out of the comfortable, cushiony bed and followed Summer obediently through the living room and on to the terrace. He scarpered off to the patch of green beyond to do his business and Summer soon lost sight of him in the murky conditions. She whistled and he came hobbling back, taking himself inside promptly while Summer remained on the terrace and breathed in the dense and misty atmosphere. It was spooky, suddenly having no view whatsoever. They were blanketed in grey. She soon realised there was little point in hanging around outside – not only was it cold and eerie, but it was quickly turning her hair into a frizz ball.

When she returned inside, she found Jude in the kitchen.

'The weather!' she said. 'It's like pea soup out there!'

'Ah, the dreaded fog. I hope my parents will be able to get in tomorrow. You know, there used to be a foghorn at the lighthouse to warn ships they were close to shallow reefs, but the powers-that-be decided it was unnecessary in this technological age. Shame, though, in a way. I can imagine there would have been something quite soothing about lying in bed here and listening to the foghorn sounding.'

'I suppose all the ships have GPS and radar nowadays. Pity, though – I'd have liked to hear it. Now, remind me, what time's the appointment today?' she asked.

Jude was now boiling the kettle and assembling two blue-and-white stripy mugs. Summer loved watching the way he made tea. It was one of her favourite things to do, observing the different way people set about making tea and then sampling the results, but with Jude it was particularly pleasing because, for a man who wasn't remotely fastidious, he was extremely methodical about tea-making.

'It's at midday. Ages away. Shall we take Prinny for a walk, or do you think we'll fall off the cliff in this weather?'

'We'll be all right. We know it like the backs of our hands now. Let's go after breakfast.'

They took their usual route, along the path behind the cottage and then up a series of steps to the cliffs – always good for the glutes. But the air was strange and moist – it seemed harder to get their breath – and when they reached the top, instead of a lovely view, they came face to face with a dead rabbit. Summer screamed as she nearly trod on it, and grabbed hold of Jude. The glassy eyes staring blindly up at them were horribly unnerving.

'It all feels like a bad omen,' Jude said eventually. 'I don't normally believe in all that sort of stuff but the weather, the rabbit . . . I've got this horrendous ball of dread sitting like a dead weight in my stomach.'

What if the tumour's ballooned and I've only got weeks, or days even, to live? I'm not ready to go, Summer. I'm just not ready.'

'Oh Jude! Come here,' said Summer, pulling him into a hug. 'Here,' she said, reaching for the long necklace she always wore, pulling it off and looping it over Jude's head.

'What does it mean, the pendant?' he asked.

'It's a Claddagh necklace. It represents love, loyalty and friendship. We moved to Ireland when I was twelve, down near Wexford, and I made friends with a wonderful Irish girl – Ciara. When we left for America when I was fourteen, she gave me this. We've always stayed in contact. And the necklace has always brought me luck. It's yours now.'

Jude touched it. 'I wondered about it . . . I thought maybe Seth had given it to you. It feels warm,' he smiled. 'The weight of it feels anchoring. It makes me feel better. Stronger.'

Summer just wished she could offer him so much more.

Jude reverted to a bag of nerves a couple of hours later, as he sat in the hospital waiting room and jiggled his leg up and down so much that another patient asked him if he'd mind cutting it out. In the end, Mr Vibert's secretary appeared, looking kindly and sympathetic.

'Would you like to follow me, Jude?'

'Shall I come with you or stay here?' Summer asked. She saw the answer in Jude's eyes immediately. He didn't want her with him when he received the news. 'I'll wait here,' she said. 'There's a gossip magazine! I can read that. Jude, good luck,' she said and she kissed him.

The next hour was agonising. Summer flicked through the pages of the magazine without registering even the pictures, let alone the sycophantic narrative accompanying them.

Then, all of a sudden, Jude reappeared in the waiting room, his face as white as a sheet. Summer's heart sank into her toes. *Oh shit.*

'What's the news?' she whispered.

'Well, the bastard tumour's there – the same as before. On the plus side, it hasn't grown any larger at this stage, which the consultant's putting down to the healthy lifestyle I've been living since I met you. I knew you were good for me, but I didn't realise quite how good!'

'Well, that's great news!' Summer smiled. 'Does that change anything?' she asked, hopefully.

'Not in itself, no. He's still giving me less than a year to live . . . Unless . . .'

Summer's eyes grew larger than ever. 'Unless?' She gripped Jude's hand.

'The consultant was telling me about some incredible advances in brain surgery across the Atlantic. It wouldn't be cheap, but there's the possibility a Canadian surgeon friend of Mr Vibert's could operate on the tumour using some cutting-edge technology not yet available in Britain. He's told me not to get my hopes up but this man – Mr Tremblay – has offered to see me. There's a small chance he may be able to operate. A tiny chance I could beat this tumour after all. Summer, I literally can't believe it. Can you pinch me?'

But Summer didn't pinch him. She rugby-tackled him into the most enormous hug and burst into loud and happy tears.

Chapter Thirty

Jersey, August

Jude

'I don't know what to do first!' Jude said, his mind spinning. They'd just got back from the hospital after stopping briefly at Waitrose to stock up on champagne. They were nervously torn between wanting to celebrate and the fear of being overly optimistic.

'It's like when you've just given birth and you really want to just recover from it all but instantly you're on the phone to everyone telling them the news. But you can't tell your parents, anyway, as they're en route, so why not give Daisy a ring and ask her to let everyone else know what's happening. Then we can get on with cracking open a bottle and making some plans.'

'*You* are full of good ideas,' Jude said, and Summer looked at him.

'You look different now, after the news,' she said. 'I've only known your beautiful face with fear casting a huge shadow over it. Now that shadow's receded slightly and I've realised you're beyond beautiful. You're devastatingly gorgeous.'

'Stop it!' Jude said, his cheeks flushing red as he squeezed Summer's hand.

When they got back, Jude rang Daisy while Summer found champagne flutes and opened the bottle, though Jude already felt fluttery and giddy, like he was drunk even though he hadn't yet had a sip. He watched Summer take her glass to the living room window and peer out of it. As if in celebration of their news, the fog had now lifted to produce, like a magic trick, a clear blue sky.

With the calls made, they took their drinks on to the terrace and toasted each other and the consultant, and prayed that Mr Tremblay in Canada would be able to help. They were exuberant. They started to gabble at each other, reflecting one moment on their fear that morning, then discussing what might happen next.

'You know – you said something before that's got me thinking,' Jude said, looking at Summer a bit shyly.

'I did?' she said, beaming.

'Uh huh. About that moment when you've just given birth. Summer, I didn't think I'd ever be a father when I received the news about the brain tumour. But now – if by any chance this guy in Canada can cure me – I'd really like us to have a baby.'

Jude watched Summer's face and thought he saw a cloud pass over it. But, 'Of course you do!' she said. 'We can discuss all that. But what else? Come on, what about everything else? Your job? Will you go back to it? Or back to teaching? Maybe it's a bit soon. How long will you need to be in Canada?'

Jude bit his lip, considering his possibilities. He realised that not everything was going to be straightforward or blissful, even should he achieve the best possible outcome in Canada. But then, that was life, wasn't it? Life in all its up-and-down glory.

Before Jude could answer her questions, Summer asked another one. 'What's the very best thing of all about this news?'

'Truthfully?'

'Of course!'

'You, Summer. The thought – the glimmer of hope – that tells me that maybe, if I'm very, very lucky, I'll have a future with you.'

Chapter Thirty-One

Jersey, August

The Party

'Jude, I've had an idea.'

'What?' Jude asked as he dried their breakfast dishes.

'Well, your parents arrive today and mine will be here shortly too. You said Daisy and Sam are keen to head over to see us this weekend as well, so why don't we throw a party? To celebrate. Or is it a bit premature?' Summer asked, anxiously.

'No, it's a brilliant idea. An opportunity to rejoice in a bit of hope, at least, and a chance to catch up with everyone before I leave for Canada next week. We can invite all my friends, and Dennis, too. We still haven't got round to having him over. Do you think you should check with Sylvie?'

'I'm sure she won't mind – she's the ultimate party animal – but I'll give her a quick call anyway, just to check in with her. We can have the party on the terrace if the weather's good. What's the forecast?'

Jude checked his phone. 'The good weather continues . . .' he smiled. 'It must be you. Is it always summer with Summer?' he asked.

'Not always,' she laughed. 'But definitely this year.'

In the afternoon, Jude and Summer walked along the lane to find Jude's parents at Dennis's holiday apartments. Summer felt ridiculously nervous but it was soon clear that, warm and polite though they were with her, their concern was not Jude's new relationship but his diagnosis. Beryl burst into tears as soon as she hugged Jude and so he quickly told them the news from his recent consultation. They were full of questions and Summer was touched to see the emerging optimism on their faces. They were exactly as she'd imagined they'd be – straightforward, humble and loving.

Eventually, Jude told them about the party.

'It won't be too grand, will it?' asked Beryl, looking concerned. 'I haven't brought anything smart to wear!'

'Not grand at all,' Summer assured her, and Beryl looked at Summer properly, as if finally able to move on to a subject other than Jude's health.

'I'm so pleased Jude met you,' Beryl told her. 'And you're just as beautiful as he said you were. But kind, too, I can see that. And that's the most important, isn't it?'

Summer adored her parents but she decided then and there that if she'd been able to have any parents other than her own, she'd have chosen Jude's.

By seven thirty on Saturday evening, the scene was set for the party. Mandla was shining like a new penny, decorated with fairy lights glittering on the terrace and some vintage bunting Summer had managed to find at a local farm shop. The cottage was shown to its best advantage in flickering candlelight.

'Are you nearly ready?' Jude asked. Summer turned to look at him. She'd been putting on what she called her 'party face', which Jude had laughed about, wondering if she was going to make herself up like a clown. Now, he looked stunned.

'Summer, you look amazing! Your eyes. I've never seen them look so . . . so . . .'

'Blue?' she giggled.

'Blue,' he agreed. 'And the dress! Is that one of your retro ones?'

'Yep! My mother's wedding dress, can you believe it?' The dress was long and strapless, made of chiffon; it was an ivory colour with enormous red poppies printed on it and was timeless in its relaxed beauty. Summer had paired it with some tan-coloured platform sandals that made her at least three inches taller. She hoped the outfit wasn't too much.

The doorbell rang.

'That'll probably be Mum and Dad,' said Jude. 'They said they'd try to get here a little early. They're over their jet lag now. Poor sods will be jet-lagged all over again next week when we head to Canada. Do you think your parents will make it in time for the party?'

'They're so vague. They were meant to be here days ago. Goodness knows what's delayed them, but they won't miss a party – believe me!'

For the next twenty minutes Summer and Jude chatted to Jude's parents, and then all of a sudden, as Summer had expected, her parents arrived in time for the party – making an entrance when their spluttering ancient camper van (the orange one Summer had driven many years before) arrived outside the cottage with a bang. Hearing the noise, Summer dragged Jude out to the front of the house with her.

'Vita! Frank!' she said as they hopped out of the van. 'Come and meet Jude!'

Jude tried to shake hands but Vita just squeezed him into an enormous hug and then Frank hugged him too, clapping him soundly on the back.

'So you're Summer's new man?' said Vita, taking him in. 'We want to hear all about how you met.'

'I'll tell you,' Summer replied. 'But first come inside and grab a drink . . .'

Jude greeted guests while Summer filled her parents in on the whole saga, finishing off with the good news about the Canadian surgeon.

'Goodness!' Vita said as she drained her first glass of fizz. 'What an adventure you've been having! I'm glad,' she admitted. 'I've always thought you were like a caged animal in that prep school. You needed to get away and actually live a little.'

'What about Seth?' Frank asked, but before Summer could answer, Daisy and Sam arrived, looking and smelling divine. Sam was introduced to Jude's parents, who seemed to take her relationship with Daisy in their stride, and then the girls caught the eye of Jude's single friends – Lee and Ben – who began a fruitless mission to seduce them. Observing the scene with an amused look on her face was Di, who looked positively regal in a long purple dress. She'd had her hair and nails done for the occasion and it was heart-warming to imagine the great care she'd gone to for a rare evening out.

'Some mango for you!' Jude said, bringing her a bowl of neatly sliced fruit he'd prepared and sitting down beside her. Summer headed over to join them.

'Oh, you angel!' Di said, immediately tucking in, using the small fork Jude had supplied. 'I adore your dog,' she said after she'd swallowed a mouthful. 'What a dear thing.' Prinny looked at her bashfully.

'Prinny, he's called. I know – he's a lovely boy. So placid.'

'I only ever 'ad a dog once. A beautiful border collie called Jess. Me 'usband Glen gave 'er to me after the war. But I was so distraught when she died some years later that I told meself I'd never get a pet again.'

'That's the only problem. Prinny has a short life expectancy too,' Jude admitted.

'Well, perhaps 'e'll defy the odds, just like you will,' Di comforted, patting Jude on the knee.

Dennis was the next to make an entrance. He was dressed in cherry-red trousers and a pale-blue shirt with buttons that strained worryingly every time he laughed – which was often. It was clear Dennis was the ultimate party guest, full of stories and keen to banter with everyone on the terrace. Summer introduced him to her parents and he seemed instantly taken with Vita, but Frank appeared entirely unfazed by Dennis's obvious pursuit. Vita had always enjoyed a bit of flattery and attention and Frank was more than happy to allow her this small pleasure. He settled down on a wooden chair with a glass of champagne and necked a couple of his pills (strictly not to be mixed with alcohol).

'Frank!' Summer said, plonking herself down next to him.

'Darling child! How are you? You're looking sensational.'

'You old charmer,' Summer laughed.

'You're in love with him, aren't you?' Frank asked as he deftly rolled a cigarette. He lit it, sheltering his lighter from the sea breeze. He inhaled, dragging on it, then exhaling. He observed Jude – who was still chatting to Di – through a haze of smoke.

Summer's eyes were drawn to Jude, too, then back to her father, who never looked any different. He'd started to go bald as a very young man so had – with some regret – cut off his long hippy locks and kept his head shaved ever since. His entire face and scalp were deeply tanned, his brow heavy and his eyes hooded, though beneath the heavy lids were eyes as blue and startling as Summer's. When he looked up it was always a little surprising to find such dazzling eyes beneath the cloak of brow and lids. Her father was the epitome of relaxed – sometimes selfishly so – but he was perceptive. He always had been.

'Completely,' Summer agreed.

'It might not work, Hoglet,' Frank said, calling Summer by the pet name he'd given her the moment she was born, when he'd decided she looked just like a baby hedgehog. 'You know – this visit to the quack in Canada.'

'Frank, he's not a quack. He's a pioneering surgeon.'

'Just . . . Hoglet, try not to get your hopes up too much. I know what you're like. Such an optimist, just like your mother. But disappointment is so crushing. I'm not saying negativity is any better, but just try to be realistic.' Frank stubbed out the cigarette in a nearby ashtray and placed a hand over Summer's.

Summer nodded, though his words weren't exactly welcome. She knew he meant well. Frank always did. And what he said made sense, of course it did. But his timing was off, as it often was. This was the party – the celebration. Realism could come later. 'Frank, I'd better go and mingle.'

'Go and break up Vita and the big guy, will you?'

Summer saw Dennis pouring Vita another glass of champagne and smiled. 'Will do!' she laughed, and she headed in their direction.

'Vita,' she said, interrupting. 'Sorry, Dennis, but she has to come and meet Jude's parents. Come on,' she said, pulling Vita away from Dennis, who looked extremely disappointed. He consoled himself with another drink and settled for Phyllis Le Feuvre, the cottage cleaner, who was a rather different proposition to Vita, with a wall eye, a floral pinafore and thick bottle-green stockings.

Summer continued to mingle and it seemed as though Jude and she were engaged in some sort of dance as they each worked the terrace, seeing to everyone else's needs, smiling at one another every so often and – eventually – finding each other again.

'It's been a success, hasn't it?' Summer said, finally reaching Jude and clinking her glass against his. The evening was still warm despite it being so late and the music and chatter created a pleasant hum. They were beside the speaker now, and one of Jude's favourite tunes began.

'Come here,' he said, and they embraced and moved gently in each other's arms as they listened to the Nothing But Thieves number, 'Last Orders'.

'It's so bleak, this song,' said Summer. 'We should be dancing to something sunnier.'

'But it's my favourite. Dark, yet there's lightness to it, too. Like my situation right now. Summer, do you think this trip to Canada's going to be worth it?'

'Whatever the outcome, it'll be worth it,' she told him. 'Because we'll know then.'

'Know what?'

'That we tried,' she said, nuzzling into Jude's shoulder. 'That we tried everything.'

Chapter Thirty-Two

Canada, September

Jude

It was a long month in a place that, in different circumstances, would have seduced Jude sufficiently to make him move there. He was like a businessman who flies to the azure shores of the Caribbean only to find himself spending the entire time in air-conditioned conference centres.

Summer didn't go with him. He'd wanted her to, but she'd said it was a journey – both literal and spiritual – that he needed to undertake with just his parents. It was agonising being apart, but within the first week he'd received the good news that – at great cost (most of which was to be met by his generous parents) – he was eligible for the operation. After that, his focus was so completely zoned in on the procedure and whether or not it would be successful that he hadn't much head space left for anything else.

Eventually the day of the operation arrived and it was pretty much a blur for Jude, as were the days that followed. He'd rather hoped that he'd immediately feel like a new man, but there were a number of gruelling side effects that struck him pretty quickly. Initially, very transient effects like a dry mouth and an incredible thirst from the breathing tube. But then there were dizzy spells, nausea, an inability to concentrate, scalp pain, exhaustion and, bizarrely, an incredibly sensitive sense of smell (he'd had to ask his father to change his socks and his mother to chew some gum). It was clear the journey was far from over.

But after a post-operative meeting with Mr Tremblay, he received the news he'd been hoping to hear. He FaceTimed Summer immediately afterwards.

'And?' Summer asked, clearly on tenterhooks. She swore she'd started to go grey since Jude had disappeared to Canada, though he couldn't see it himself – her hair looked as dark and lustrous as usual.

'It's been a success!' Jude told her. 'I mean, the medics are *very* cautious about calling it a cure, as brain tumours are notoriously cockroach-like in their tendency to reappear, but with this technology the surgeon used he was able to get rid of the tumour completely and, as far as he can tell, all cancerous cells.'

'Jude, that's incredible! I'm so happy! And, for the record, your head looks pretty amazing shaved. You look like Wentworth Miller from *Prison Break*!'

Jude laughed. 'Apart from all the metal staples! My equivalent to his tattoos, maybe!'

'So what happens next?' Summer asked, her eyes bright with excitement. Before he could reply, Vita and Frank appeared on screen.

'We've been sending you good vibes!' Vita called. 'So, so happy it's worked! Frank's got some fantastic painkillers for you if you need them when you get back, haven't you, darling?'

'Totally,' Frank agreed. 'Ace news, mate. Completely cool. Summer's been a nightmare. I've never known her so tetchy.' Summer thumped Frank on the arm.

'Bugger off!' she told them now and they vanished, chuckling as they drifted off to another room. 'Sorry about that!'

'No probs,' said Jude. 'But I can't remember what you asked me now! That keeps happening. I get halfway through a sentence and I've no idea what I was going to say next. Apparently it's normal.'

'Sounds like me on a good day!' Summer laughed. 'I just wondered what's going to happen next?' she asked again.

'The surgeon reckons I'll be well enough to fly about a week from now, so we're going to book the return flights once we know for sure. Once I'm back in Jersey it'll be a question of taking it easy for a while and having regular check-ups, just to make sure the tumour doesn't reappear. But the surgeon's "cautiously optimistic".'

'And how are you feeling? You look great!'

'More side effects than I'd expected, but over the next few months I should gradually start to feel better and, with any luck, I won't be struck down with any more horrendous headaches.'

'Oh Jude! It's just so unbelievable! Let me know as soon as you have a date for your return and I'll start getting everything ready for a hero's welcome.'

'A hero? Hardly! But thank you, Summer. I've missed you so much.'

'Me too,' Summer agreed. 'No more partings, okay? I can't take any more!'

Jude laughed. 'Promise,' he said, and a week later, as hoped, he returned.

Chapter Thirty-Three

Jersey, November

Summer

Jude's recovery was slow. Three steps forward, two steps back, just as Mr Tremblay had predicted. Summer was there for him throughout this period and after a couple of months he was a lot stronger. His hair had grown a little, too, so the staples were less visible. As soon as he'd returned in September, Vita and Frank had said their goodbyes, unusually tactful. They'd left their van at Mandla and booked themselves flights to India, where they planned to meet up with Sylvie. Jude's parents had returned to Australia in early October and finally he and Summer were alone again.

During the recovery period, by some kind of unspoken agreement, Jude and Summer lived very much in the moment, neither quite ready to discuss the future until they could be sure Jude really was improving. But in November, Jude went to see Mr Vibert for a further scan and was given a cautious all-clear – he would have to return for scans at six-month intervals, as no one seemed to trust these brain tumours. Also, Summer couldn't ignore for much longer the fact that her six-month marital break was almost at an end.

After the scan, in the evening, they lit the log burner and opened a bottle of champagne to celebrate Jude's news. Summer was sitting at his feet by the fire when he posed the question she'd been expecting.

'When are you going to tell Seth?' he asked.

'Oh, I . . . I can't quite decide. Maybe tomorrow?'

'You don't sound too sure.'

'I'm just . . . I mean, I know I was always going to end it with him, and I know the six-month break is nearly over, but it's just . . . I'm not sure how to explain . . .'

'What's the problem? You were going to finish with Seth and be alone so surely it's easier to end things now you know you're going to be with me?' Jude asked.

'I guess it's just that we have so much history – the boys, for one thing. I know he's been having an affair with Barbara and obviously I've been with you but, despite everything, it's still a big deal . . .'

Jude looked stung, as if Summer's words were a slap round the face. 'Well, don't let me stop you going back to him if it's too big a deal! Have I been really stupid here? Did you never actually plan to leave him at all? Perhaps you were just going to have your fun with me, then head back when the six-month break was over.' His voice was hoarse with emotion.

'No, Jude, of course not!' Summer cried, but it was clear Jude was now deaf to any reasoning she might try. 'Wait!' she shouted as Jude stormed towards the kitchen. He left, letting the front door slam in the age-old tradition of domestics.

Summer felt awful. To have ruined everything with her hesitance about contacting Seth to finish things for good. But she also felt a little concerned about seeing this other side of Jude – she'd never experienced him storming off like a child before, without giving her a chance to explain. She felt bad, but she also felt angry.

And anyway, he was wrong. She was well and truly over Seth. She wanted nothing more than to be with Jude, but severing a relationship of more than twenty years *was* a big deal. Why couldn't he understand that? But then he'd never had a long-term relationship, had he? He couldn't even begin to imagine what it was like.

The whole situation was horribly unsettling, but Summer's worries didn't end there. At the back of her mind was something else that Jude had mentioned the very first day Mr Vibert had given him hope by telling him about his surgeon friend in Canada. He wanted a baby, he'd told her – *If by any chance this guy in Canada can cure me – I'd really like to have a baby*, he'd said.

But Summer knew, without a shadow of a doubt, that she didn't ever want to have another child.

Chapter Thirty-Four

JERSEY, NOVEMBER

JUDE

He thought he'd drive back to his own flat and spend the night there, but then realised he'd had far too much to drink. Instead, he took his trainers off and left them by his car and then stumbled through the icy darkness towards the beach, guided only by the moonlight. He reached the bay and came upon an illuminated rock. He sat on it and finally his breathing began to steady. He could hear the gentle swoosh of the incoming tide, but other than that there was no noise. The beach felt different at night. It was like being on another planet.

He closed his eyes and breathed in deeply. A salty, seaweedy scent that soothed and sobered him. Perhaps his reaction had been an inevitable outcome of such a highly charged day. Jude thought about it now and realised he'd been quite unreasonable.

Of course it was going to be hard for Summer to cut all ties with Seth after twenty years together. It was his inherent insecurity getting the better of him, making him jump to stupid conclusions. He was ashamed of himself. But then, perhaps in some strange way it had been a good thing – to have a row of sorts. There was always going to be a first time and now it was done. Over. Though the longer he stayed out there, the longer it would continue in Summer's mind. He must get back to her. Make it all better. Jude jumped up and ran all the way back to the cottage. He found Summer propped up in bed, reading her book. Her face – make-up free and wearing her rather battered glasses – looked touchingly vulnerable.

'Summer, I'm so sorry,' Jude said immediately. 'I don't know what I was thinking. I was being pathetic and insecure and a little bit drunk. Forgive me?' he asked.

Summer looked hurt. 'Jude, you didn't even hear me out. It wasn't fair . . .'

'I know. I'm so ashamed of myself.' Jude hung his head. After a moment, Summer sighed.

'The truth is,' she said, 'I don't know why I haven't told Seth already, other than I know it's going to open a can of worms and all be terribly dramatic and I don't want that to impinge on our celebrations.'

'Then don't tell him yet. Let's just enjoy the next few days and you can speak to him when you're ready. I'm not going to mention it again.'

'Good,' Summer said, smiling at last. Jude joined her in bed then, and it was all quickly forgotten. He stuck to his word and didn't raise the subject again.

But in the end the matter was taken out of Summer's hands, for six months to the day after she'd left for Jersey in May, she received a telephone call from Seth.

Chapter Thirty-Five

Jersey, November

Summer

'Summer,' he said.

'Seth, hi,' she replied. She felt as awkward as a teenager about to dump her first boyfriend.

'Oh my goodness, it's so lovely to hear your voice!' Seth said warmly. He proceeded to chatter on, barely drawing breath as he told her about various goings-on at the school and in the village. Eventually, of course, the conversation moved on to the subject of them. 'I've missed you, Summer. It's been awful not being able to contact you. But it's been a good thing, too. It's made me think. I know now, Summer, that I don't want to lose you. When are you coming home?'

Summer was taken aback. What about Barbara? Perhaps it had fizzled out. This was a scenario she somehow hadn't quite expected. She'd imagined Seth feeling similarly to her or being indifferent. But not this. Not a warm, chatty and remorseful Seth, ready and willing, eager even, to give their marriage another go.

'Seth, it's not that simple. I've . . . I've met someone. Over here, in Jersey.'

There was silence. Eventually: 'You've met someone?' Seth sounded utterly dumbfounded. 'You mean a man?'

Summer almost wanted to laugh at how implausible Seth seemed to think this was. She tried not to feel insulted.

'Yes, a man.'

'Good golly. Well, I wasn't expecting that. But I understand . . . It's my fault. I shouldn't have suggested the break – of course you'd have ended up having some sort of rebound fling. I forgive you.'

'You *forgive* me!' Summer felt her cheeks burning. 'What about you and Barbara?'

'What on earth do you mean?'

So he was going to deny it. How ridiculous. 'Oh, for heaven's sake, Seth.'

'Look, I don't know what Barbara's got to do with this, but let's get your return sorted out and we'll deal with everything once you're here. Have you booked your flight?'

This was going to be harder than expected. Summer took a deep breath. 'No, Seth, I haven't booked my flight. And I'm not planning to. I've fallen in love. And I'm not coming home.' She paused, took another breath. Silence. 'Seth?'

But the line had gone dead.

Chapter Thirty-Six

Jersey, November

Jude

'I guessed it was Seth! How'd it go?' Jude asked with a sympathetic look as Summer came to find him huddled up in a thick jacket on the terrace. Prinny was dozing at his feet and he had a gin and tonic in one hand and the local newspaper, which was fluttering wildly, in the other.

'Not great. He put the phone down on me! I rang the boys afterwards and they were sad, though understanding. They didn't think the marriage would have legs after a six-month break anyway, especially as I'd told them about you and, of course, about Barbara. I spoke to Tilly, too, and explained the situation. She was really pleased for me! She's going to pop round to the bungalow to find some of my winter clothes to post over.'

'Retro stuff?'

'No, all the retro things I used to wear of my mum's were mainly summery. My headmaster's wife wardrobe is terribly dull by comparison, but at least I'll be warm.'

'How are you feeling? Actually, don't tell me yet. I'm freezing. Can we go back inside and get you a drink and then you can tell me?'

Summer laughed. 'Good idea!'

'So?' Jude asked ten minutes later as they thawed by the fire, drinks in hand.

'Relieved, that's how I feel. Totally relieved.'

'Me too. Summer, this is it. We can be a couple now. A proper couple. We can shout it from the rooftops if we want to. Actually, that's not really my style, but you know what I mean. And I know I've mentioned this before, but we haven't discussed it properly yet. Summer, let's have a baby together,' Jude said eagerly.

'Oh Jude, you're serious, aren't you?'

'Of course,' he said. 'Summer, don't you feel the same?'

'I love *you*, Jude. I love you more than anything. But I don't want any more kids. I've been there, done that.'

'Sure, with Seth. Not with me. Summer, please. You may not feel like having them right away, but in the next couple of years, maybe?'

Summer shifted uncomfortably on the sofa. She bit her lip, then looked at Jude, and he realised then that she was completely and utterly against the idea.

'You really don't want any more kids?' he asked.

'Never,' Summer whispered. 'I never want any more children.'

Chapter Thirty-Seven

Jersey, November

Summer

'Please, Summer,' Jude tried again. 'This is a massive issue for me. Maybe Seth wasn't very helpful, but I would be. I'll do everything, if you'll just agree . . . Feeding, nappies, everything . . .'

Poor Jude. He sounded desperate, but Summer was resolute. 'Absolutely not.'

'Okay, just one then. One child.'

'No!'

'Summer, you're being so rigid about this. I don't understand!'

Summer was silent. She tried to summon up the words to explain. But she couldn't. And by the time she'd mustered up the courage, she saw Jude had disappeared from the room. The front door slammed loudly, just as it had after their first row. She felt angry, again, at this petulant attitude of his, which seemed to highlight his immaturity as far as relationships were concerned. Again, he hadn't given her a chance to explain.

This time, though, Jude didn't return swiftly. The next morning, Summer awoke to find an empty space beside her in the bed. She felt sick. She would explain everything the very moment Jude got back. It was just so hard to talk about. But she needed to, she realised. She couldn't keep him in the dark any longer. By ten there was still no sign of Jude, and Prinny really needed his walk. It was raining – a thick and heavy downpour – and Prinny didn't look that keen, but it was important he had his daily exercise to keep his muscles supple. Summer also remembered that she and Jude were meant to be taking their first ballet lesson that morning, so she rang Madame Vivier to cancel it.

The phone call made, she found a raincoat she'd been borrowing from Jude and trudged along the path behind the cottage and up the steps to the cliffs. She hadn't felt much like walking, but the exercise was reviving and she found herself feeling better. All she needed to do was tell Jude everything and he'd understand, she was sure. She walked briskly on the way back, full of determination. If he wasn't there when she got home, she'd call him immediately on his mobile and arrange to meet him somewhere.

There was no sign of his car. Summer discarded her muddy trainers outside the front door and let herself into the kitchen, shrugging off the raincoat and letting Prinny past, who slurped noisily at his water before collapsing into his bed.

She hung the coat on the back of a kitchen chair to drip-dry and it was only then she noticed that a fresh bunch of anemones had been placed in a terracotta jug on the table. Strange. They definitely hadn't been there before.

'Jude!' she called out, heading into the living room, but there was no reply.

She returned to the kitchen and saw that her Claddagh necklace was beside the jug, and tucked underneath it was a note. She opened it, her hands trembling.

Summer,

You've been the best thing that's ever happened to me and I could never have got through these months without you. In some incredible way you made the most difficult period in my life also the very happiest. But perhaps we were never meant to be together for ever. We've been carrying on with one another since the good news, hoping for the best. But with a future ahead of us, it seems as though we want totally different things, and I can't bear the thought of those differing desires slowly tearing us apart. What we had deserves better than that. I'm heading to the airport now, to London, and then to Perth to be with my parents for a bit. I know it's all quite sudden, but – believe me – I did nothing but think and plan and pack all night.

Summer, you should go back to Seth if it's over with him and Barbara. You've got so much history. Much as it galls me to say it, I don't think you should throw all that away. I know he doesn't like dogs or he's allergic or something, so I thought perhaps you could ask Dennis to look after Prinny for a while, just until I'm sure whether I'm going to stay in Australia or not? I'm sorry to lumber you with the arrangements, but I haven't time to speak to him before I leave. Give the boy a big cuddle from me (Prinny, not Dennis!) and remember, Summer, that whatever happens, I'll always love you.

Jude

PART FOUR

FALLING IN LOVE AGAIN

DECEMBER 2017–DECEMBER 2018

Chapter Thirty-Eight

England, December

Summer

Summer heaved the groceries out of the car and bundled the Tesco bags into the hallway. She returned to the car to lock it and realised she could hear the school choir practising carols in the theatre. For some reason, the sound of 'Silent Night' made her want to cry. She hurried back inside and turned on the TV in the kitchen to drown out the innocent voices and the melancholy music. She unpacked the shopping then took the bag of toiletries and loo roll through to the bathroom. She closed the door and pulled the packet she needed out of the carrier bag. She stared at it for a while, though she knew exactly how to use it. She'd used enough of the things last time around, just to be sure.

It was digital, though, in this day and age, and there was no chance of trying to analyse whether a second line was appearing as the minutes ticked by. Instead, there was just some stupid picture of an egg timer. She sat on the edge of the bath and closed her eyes, replaying all the events that had happened since the day she'd received Jude's note.

She'd tried calling him, of course. Immediately. But he'd turned off his phone. Then she'd sped off to the airport in the camper van. But she was too late. Frustratingly, the plane was still there, but the gate was closed and there was no persuading the man she'd collared to pass a message on to one of the passengers.

She'd returned to Mandla and tried Daisy next. Sam had picked up and explained Daisy was working. She didn't know anything about Jude heading to London and Summer could only assume Jude was flying straight to Perth from Gatwick rather than stopping off with his sister.

Finally, she'd FaceTimed Jude's parents.

'Will you get him to call me?' Summer had asked them. 'It's just . . . There's things I need to explain to him.'

'Of course we will, dear. Now don't you worry,' Beryl had comforted. 'I'm sure it'll all blow over. A storm in a teacup.'

But Jude hadn't called and the next time Summer had tried to FaceTime David and Beryl, there'd been no answer.

She'd given up. Feeling numb, she'd rung Seth, who was – to give him his due – gracious about the whole thing. She'd booked a flight, packed and delivered Prinny to Dennis, sobbing as she'd walked back to Mandla alone. She'd left the cottage tidy.

Seth had welcomed her home warmly. She'd thought it would all be horribly awkward but, for some reason, it hadn't been. She was heartbroken, and in some strange way Seth felt like a remedy.

On her first evening back at Headmaster's House, Summer had asked about Barbara.

'It was nothing,' Seth said, looking uncomfortable. 'Look, I don't want to drag it all up with you any more than you probably want to talk about this man you met in Jersey. Whatever happened in those six months, perhaps we both needed it. Now I think it's time to move on. What do you say?'

'I think that's a very good idea,' she'd agreed. She'd far rather not talk about Jude – it was too painful to think about him, let alone talk about what had happened. And she was quite happy to dismiss all thoughts of Barbara Robinson, too. Seth was right: those six months were just a – for her, magical – period in time and, now that they were back together, it was important to move on.

Summer had turned towards Seth that night, in bed, and for the first time in a very long while they'd sought comfort in each other. She'd even wondered, as she lay in his arms, if she was falling in love with him again.

Now, it was two weeks later, and the three minutes were up. Summer looked at the test. 'Pregnant', it screamed at her. She lifted the lavatory lid and instantly threw up.

Chapter Thirty-Nine

ENGLAND, DECEMBER

SUMMER

'I'm sorry,' Tilly said. 'I thought you just said you're pregnant!'

'I did,' Summer replied as she cradled her mug of tea in her hands. She was sitting at Tilly's kitchen table, while her friend went about her baking. She was hoping to get into the *Great British Bake Off* and was endlessly practising cakes and scones and breads, much to the pleasure of everyone around her. Apart from Summer, who felt sick even smelling the freshly baked cakes.

'But . . .' Tilly looked shocked. 'But you can't be!'

Summer laughed. 'Tilly, you've gone quite pale. Don't worry – the baby's not yours!' But she knew why Tilly looked so horrified – she knew all about Summer's phobia.

'Who's the father?' she asked.

Summer shifted uncomfortably. 'Um, that's the problem. Or one of the problems, anyway. I don't know. I feel like I should be some slutty character in *EastEnders* or something, but I honestly don't know if it's Seth's or Jude's. You know I told you I'd met someone, when you offered to send over my winter clothes? Jude was my reason for staying and – well, it's a long story but, as you've probably guessed, he was also my reason for coming home.'

'Yes, I gathered something must have gone a bit wrong. But goodness, Summer,' she said, sounding quite exasperated. 'I know you're a scatterbrain, but I'd have thought you'd have learnt your lesson on the contraception front after a teenage pregnancy!'

'Believe me, I did. But Jude and I had this one occasion, a few nights before he left, where the, um . . .' It was all a bit crude to discuss. 'We slipped up, shall we say? And then, when I got back, I wasn't expecting anything to happen with Seth. We hadn't had sex for over eighteen months, so we weren't quite prepared. I was planning to go to the doctor's to get myself sorted out this week, then I realised. My period was late.'

'So it wasn't just a one-off with Seth?' Tilly asked.

'I thought it might be, but . . .' Summer blushed. 'I guess we're kind of rediscovering one another.'

'What about this other chap then?' Tilly asked, carefully balancing one layer of sponge on top of another as if her life depended on it.

'I'm just trying not to think about him, truthfully. But now . . . Well, I don't know what to do. Shall I just come clean and tell them both?'

'No. No, don't do that. I hate to say it, but it's early days still, isn't it? Why not just wait until the first scan? Make sure everything's okay. Then tell them. What will you do, assuming all is fine with the baby? Will you stay with Seth? Or go back to Jude?'

'Tilly, you've forgotten the third option.'

'Which is?'

'Do it all alone. Let's face it, do you really think either of them is going to be interested in bringing up a child that may or may not be theirs?'

'Good point,' Tilly agreed a little too readily, and Summer found herself feeling a bit hurt that her friend hadn't offered her a 'congratulations', even if the circumstances weren't ideal.

Later, at dinner, Seth offered Summer a glass of wine as they sat opposite each other at the table. The smell of steak rising from Seth's plate was making Summer want to heave.

'No thanks, I'll stick to water. Still feel a bit funny. Can't seem to shake off this bug.'

Seth looked at her across the table, his face solemn. 'Summer, when were you going to tell me?'

'Tell you what?' she asked, her heart pounding.

'That you're pregnant.'

'How . . . how do you know?'

'You mustn't be cross with her, but Tilly told me.'

'Tilly? But . . .' Summer was speechless. How could her friend betray her in such a way?

'She's worried about you. About the phobia. She thought I might be able to help you.'

'But Seth, did she tell you? I don't know if the baby's yours.'

'I know. And we'll get a paternity test done, just as soon as it's born. I'm quite prepared to be a father again, though not to a baby that's not mine. I do have my limits,' he half-laughed. 'But for now, until we know, I'll try to help. I know this must be hard for you. Do you want to talk about it?'

Summer's eyes filled with tears. 'No,' she told him. 'Not yet. I can't even think about – you know . . . the birth,' she whispered.

'Poor Summer,' said Seth and he reached across the table and rubbed her hand.

Chapter Forty

England, December

Summer

The following day Summer nipped round to Tilly's. She knew her friend would have had her best interests at heart, telling Seth about the baby, but she wanted to have it out with her regardless. After all, she'd been the one to advise Summer not to tell Seth or Jude until after the first scan.

She let herself in the back door, as she always did, but there was no sign of Tilly in the kitchen. Ken Bruce burbled on from the radio and she could smell scones baking in the Aga. Tilly must be around somewhere. Summer went through the kitchen door into the grand entrance hall, and was about to shout for her friend when she heard urgent voices coming from the sitting room.

'Did you tell her?' Tilly was saying. 'Did you finish things?'

'I know I said yesterday that I would, but when it came to it I couldn't do it. Tilly, I can't just ditch her now. She's so vulnerable. But I told her I'll leave if the baby's not mine.'

'*If* the baby's not yours? But what if it is? Don't tell me you're going to stay? After everything . . . Seth, I know you wanted Summer to come back after your break when I wouldn't leave Angus, but I've told him now. I've filed for a divorce, for heaven's sake! I've sacrificed a lot so that we can be together. You can't now backtrack just because of some unplanned child that may not even be yours!'

Summer put a hand to her mouth. Seth and Tilly? It made no sense! She'd always thought they loathed each other. But then, perhaps that had all been a cover? What a fool she'd been. She made to run away, but then stopped in her tracks. No. She would face this head-on. She walked calmly, almost regally, into the sitting room. Two faces looked at her, aghast.

'How long?' Summer asked simply. 'How long has this been going on?'

That evening, Summer began to pack – again. She'd called Sylvie immediately after the revelation and Sylvie had kindly agreed Summer could return to Mandla as she had no immediate plans to return from India and she never let the place during the winter. When she'd been with Jude, Summer had often imagined Mandla at Christmas, the log burner flaming, a bedecked tree in the corner of the living room, fairy lights casting a mellow glow on the beautiful cottage.

But now the prospect of Christmas there alone filled her with a bleak and dismal dread. She'd called the boys after ringing Sylvie, to tell them the news and ask if they'd like to join her there, but they'd reminded her that they'd already planned a ski trip with their mates and, although they'd offered to cancel it, she didn't want to ruin their fun. And at least she had a place to go. There was no way she could spend another moment within a hundred yards of Seth or Tilly.

Five years, they'd told her. For five years they'd been having an affair right under her nose. She couldn't understand it. If they'd wanted to be together, why not just end things with Summer and Angus and set up with one another? The reason, it turned out, was mercenary. Angus, who was very careful with his (many) pennies, had insisted on a pre-nuptial agreement before he and Tilly married. He'd wanted to protect his enormous family wealth. To leave him to be with Seth would have meant a dramatic change in living standards that Tilly hadn't been pre-pared to make. Or at least, not for a long while. She'd had the clever idea of Seth suggesting the break with Summer to coincide with Angus being away doing his pilot training, so that she and Seth could spend that time together, even though – at that point – she'd still had no inten-tion of leaving Angus altogether.

But then, when Summer returned from Jersey, it had made Tilly realise just how much she wanted Seth for herself, regardless of the money. She'd filed for divorce from Angus and the very next day it had all come out. That, contrary to what Seth had told Tilly, he and Summer had reignited their relationship and – what's more – she was pregnant with, potentially, his child. No wonder Tilly had looked so pale and horrified when Summer had told her the news.

It had all been quite a shock, particularly Seth's words when he'd seen Summer starting to pack.

'If you leave, Summer, you'd better be warned that I'll want nothing to do with that baby, whether it's mine or not.'

Summer hadn't dignified this with a response. What was it? A threat? Did he really still want her to stay? Perhaps he simply couldn't make up his mind between the two of them. Well, she would make his mind up for him.

But it had been an extremely stressful day, heaped on top of Summer's anxiety that she was pregnant. And it now looked very much like she was going to have to deal with it all alone.

Chapter Forty-One

Jersey, December

Summer

Christmas Eve and it was icy-cold. Summer was snuggled on the sofa with Prinny, the fire roaring and a blanket heaped on top of them both. In an effort to make herself feel festive she'd strung fairy lights over the mirror in the living room and had even, at the last minute, bought a small tree from the central market. Only after she'd heaved it home and put it up had she realised she didn't actually have any decorations and she'd had to get back in the orange camper van and hotfoot it to St Aubin before early closing time, where she'd found a small gift shop selling overpriced baubles and more strings of lights. Experiencing the bustle around her had actually buoyed her up a little and she'd decorated the tree listening to carols on the radio and even managed not to cry when the choir sang 'Silent Night'.

She ate pizza for supper and settled down to watch something on the TV. *Bridget Jones's Diary* was on, which would do nicely. Ten minutes in, her phone pinged. A text. She read it, then, disbelieving, read it again.

I would say meet me at the lighthouse, but it's cold and dark and, as it's Christmas Eve, you've probably got other plans. But I know you're in Jersey and if by any chance you're still talking to me, I'd love to see you. If I don't hear from you, I'll understand. Merry Christmas, Summer! Love Jude

Summer gulped, her heart racing. Jude was here. In Jersey. Had he come here specially to see her? Was he here anyway, returned from Australia? And how did he know she was back? So many questions ran through her mind but there was only going to be one way she'd find out the answers. She called him on her mobile, her hands shaking.

'Jude? It's me, Summer,' she said apprehensively.

'Summer,' he said, and to hear his voice was how it must be for a reformed drug addict suddenly offered narcotics during their recovery process. A large part of her was still angry with him at having given up on her so easily, especially when she'd been there for him throughout his illness, but it still felt wonderful to hear his voice again. 'I'm so pleased you rang. I got back this morning.'

'From Australia?'

'No, Camford. Summer, I've been completely at a loss without you. I travelled back from Oz a week ago, saw Daisy briefly and then went in search of you. I tracked down the school you'd told me about and bumped straight into Seth, literally. He told me you'd gone back to him, but then changed your mind and headed to Jersey.'

'Did he say anything else?' Summer asked carefully.

'No, I didn't hang around. He looked a bit glum. He had a grocery bag with him, which he dropped when we bumped into each other. It had a bottle of wine in it and a sorry-looking microwave meal for one. I guess he's missing you.'

'Not me. My friend, Tilly.'

'What do you mean?'

'Look, there's so much to talk about. I don't suppose you fancy coming round now, do you? I'm all alone, apart from Prinny, and I'm fairly sure he'll be glad to see you.' She wanted to have it out with him and it seemed a better idea to do it in person.

'I can't think of anything I'd love more,' Jude told her. 'I'm at the flat. I can be with you in twenty minutes or so . . . But listen, I can't wait any longer to tell you how sorry I am. Leaving the way I did – it was so cowardly of me. I've been thinking so much about Granny Sabine and Di and the war years. They'd never have behaved like I did – giving up so easily. I feel ashamed of myself.'

'You didn't give me a chance to explain, that's what got to me. You stormed off like a kid, Jude, and I can't be dealing with that. We're adults. We have to communicate.'

'I know,' Jude said sorrowfully. 'I've realised that the fact I've never been in love before has worked to my disadvantage – I'm a rookie at this love stuff. I need Learner plates.'

Summer laughed at last. 'Yes,' she said. 'Yes, you do!'

'So can I still come round?' Jude asked tentatively.

'Yes, but I'm not making any promises. We need to talk some more.'

'I'll take that,' said Jude. 'Summer, I've missed you so much.'

Summer hesitated then sighed, unable to pretend. 'I've missed you too, Jude,' she admitted. She wondered how she was going to feel when she saw him. Would she feel like forgiving him as soon as she saw his face, or would she find that her feelings for him had changed once she saw him in the flesh? Either way, she would find out soon enough.

Chapter Forty-Two

Jersey, December

Jude

To see Summer and Prinny snuggled up by the fire on Christmas Eve in Mandla was like being in one of the dreams Jude had enjoyed on a regular basis when he'd been in Australia – dreams so sweet he would try to force himself back to sleep in the hope that his imaginary world would carry on where it had left off.

When she saw him, Summer paused whatever she'd been watching on TV and there was a moment of quiet between them – the only sound the low rumble of someone talking on the radio in the kitchen. Summer jumped up and they embraced for a long time, until she started to cry.

'What's up?' Jude asked anxiously. 'Don't cry. Come on, let's have a drink. Have you got a bottle open?'

Summer shook her head. Jude thought she must still be cross with him and he couldn't blame her. Perhaps she didn't want him to stay long enough for a drink.

But suddenly she looked at him in despair. 'I'm pregnant, Jude,' she blurted out.

Jude could feel the blood draining from his face. He didn't know whether to feel happy or shocked – a combination of elation and concern competed with each other in his mind. 'But . . . but you didn't want any more children,' he whispered, sitting down on the sofa with a thump. Summer sat down next to him.

'I know. It wasn't planned, obviously.'

'Was it that time, just before I left?'

'Possibly . . . though . . . Jude, this is so awful to have to tell you, but the baby might be Seth's. We started up our relationship again when I went back to him. There's a chance it could be his.'

Jude felt the joy from a moment before diminish instantly. He felt physically sick. He puffed his cheeks then let out a whistle. 'Wow!' was all he could manage to say. He took Summer's hand in his. 'Then why aren't you with him now?' he asked, confused. 'Actually, don't answer that yet. I need a drink. Let's go through to the kitchen and I'll make you a cup of tea and find myself something stronger.'

Jude led the way to the kitchen and put the kettle on, while Summer sat at the table looking nervous. He rummaged around and found a bottle of brandy, pouring himself a hefty tot.

'There are mince pies if you want one,' Summer offered, but Jude had never felt less hungry. He made Summer's tea and then took their drinks to the table, sitting down opposite her. He realised she'd never looked more beautiful – pregnancy clearly suited her, even if she hadn't wanted this baby.

'So what happened with Seth?' Jude asked, taking a restoring sip of brandy with a slightly shaking hand.

'I only went back to him because I thought you never wanted to see me again,' Summer explained. 'When you left, I followed you to the airport, I contacted your parents, I tried calling you . . . It was clear you didn't want to speak to me. I was so hurt by that, Jude. It felt like you threw away what we had so easily. I thought I'd found the love of my life and then – just like that – you were gone. And Seth, I knew, wanted me back. So I went. I did what you suggested in your note. He's always represented security for me and that's what I felt I needed right then, more than anything. He was a comfort when my heart was breaking. Then, before I knew it, I discovered I was pregnant, which was a bombshell in itself. I didn't know what to do. Then there was another bombshell.'

'Blimey! What else?' Jude wasn't sure he could take much more. He threw back the rest of the brandy then replenished his glass from the bottle beside him.

'I found out Seth's been having an affair with my friend Tilly for the last five years!'

Jude's eyes widened. 'You're kidding! I thought he was having it off with that woman called Barbara. But why did he want you to go back to him, then? After the break?'

Summer's cheeks reddened and Jude realised how angry she must be with the pair of them. 'Barbara was a decoy. Tilly just made it all up. Apparently, Tilly had told Seth she wouldn't leave her husband, Angus, for him. He's loaded and she has a prenup with him so she won't receive any of his money if she leaves him. But then, when I returned, I think it made her realise how much she wanted Seth after all. So she filed for divorce with Angus. The very next day I told her I was pregnant, that Seth and I had rekindled our relationship. As you can imagine, she was horrified. Seth had obviously kept her in the dark about that. So I left as quickly as I could after I found out about the affair, and fortunately Sylvie said I could use the cottage again.'

'And what about Seth and Tilly now? Are they together?'

'I've no idea, though you said Seth had a microwave meal for one, which makes me think Tilly hasn't quite forgiven him yet.'

'What a betrayal . . . Summer, I'm so sorry. What a mess you're in. Does Seth know about the baby?'

'Yes, and he's not interested. But Jude, I haven't even told you the worst of it yet.'

'There's more?' Jude's mind was in turmoil as he tried to take it all in.

'There is. You know I told you I didn't ever want any more children? Well, that's not strictly true. I love kids. I adore babies. I'd have lots more in an ideal world. Especially with you. But I had such a traumatic birth with the twins. I ended up with an emergency C-section and a general anaesthetic so I didn't even see them being born, and then a blood transfusion. I came this close to losing my life,' she said, pinching her index finger and thumb together. 'It's not just that I'm mentally scarred by what happened. I've actually been diagnosed as having a severe phobia. Secondary tokophobia, it's called. Fear of childbirth.'

'But why on earth didn't you tell me?' Jude asked, looking aghast. He couldn't believe she hadn't felt able to tell him about the phobia – it would have explained so much and saved them such a lot of pain.

'You didn't give me a chance – I was about to tell you when you ran away! And I'd wanted to tell you before then, too – as soon as I realised you wanted children. I kept planning on telling you. It's just such a hard topic for me to discuss. I get into quite a state even thinking about the birth I had with Luke and Levi. And now . . . Oh Jude, I'm absolutely terrified.'

'You don't need to be. We'll look into counselling or something. Cat might know where we can get help – we'll ask her . . . And I'll be with you throughout, just as you were there for me throughout my illness. I'll help you through the pregnancy, the birth, everything. I'll be there, Summer. I know you'll be worried that I'll be off again at the first sign of trouble, but I honestly won't be. I'm so sorry I left you, but I promise you now, I won't ever leave you again.'

'But Jude, what if the baby's not yours?'

'It *will* be mine, whether or not it's mine genetically. Look, I know this is going to be hard for you, but for me it really is the best news ever. We're going to have a baby together. And I'll help you through it, Summer. I promise. Hey, listen, this is a sign.'

'What is?'

'This song. On the radio. "Have Yourself a Merry Little Christmas". It's my favourite. It's the original one too, the Judy Garland one.'

Summer listened to the soothing tune and the comforting lyrics – she just wished her own troubles could be out of sight by the following year.

'Why's it your favourite?' Summer asked, with a watery smile.

'It's nice and gentle. Not too jingly! Summer, we'll get through this together. I know we will.'

The song finished.

'What do you think?' Jude asked Summer, holding out a hand to her. 'Do you forgive me? Can we try again . . . as a family this time?'

Summer nodded. 'Yes,' she whispered. 'Let's do this.'

Chapter Forty-Three

Jersey, July

Summer

The baby was due in August, but in the middle of the night in July – six weeks before her due date – Summer realised something wasn't right. Her back was aching, the kind of aching she'd only experienced once before, when she'd been in labour with the boys.

This wasn't the plan, but Summer had been having one-to-one hypno-birthing lessons with a brilliant midwife recommended by Cat, who'd worked wonders with her phobia and reinstated her faith in the birthing process, and Jude had been incredibly supportive, constantly researching the best ways to deal with tokophobia. So, although she hadn't been expecting to go into labour so early, she managed to keep a cool head.

'Jude!' Summer called out in the darkness. 'Jude, I think I'm in labour!'

'You can't be!' he said, turning on his bedside light.

'I'm sure of it.'

'Has it only just started?'

'Yes, but we'd better get to the hospital before too long as it's so early. I was so hoping for a home birth as well!'

'You can still do everything we planned. We'll make sure we repeat all your affirmations and we'll ask for a water birth and to keep the lights dim . . . Let me get everything together – all the aromatherapy and stuff . . .'

Jude jumped out of bed. He was clearly trying to stay calm for Summer, but he looked a bit panic-stricken as he raced around the cottage throwing things into a bag. Summer concentrated on the breathing techniques she'd learnt and was amazed at how effective they were. She knew fear was her enemy and that she needed to try to keep adrenaline at bay so that the oxytocin could do its work and allow a straightforward and hopefully speedy labour.

'Do you want to have a shower or anything while I let Prinny out and give him some food?' Jude asked a few minutes later.

'Okay, maybe a bath, actually . . .' said Summer, and she lay for some time in the warm water, candles flickering as she focused on her breath and listened to the hypno-birthing download she'd been given by the midwife.

By the time they reached the hospital, it was two hours after it had all begun. Summer continued to focus on her breathing while Jude explained her history to the on-duty midwife, who examined Summer and told her she was sufficiently dilated to get into the water. She went off to get the pool ready while Jude stroked Summer's back.

'I can't believe you're six centimetres dilated,' Jude murmured. 'You're doing amazingly.'

Summer smiled, enjoying a momentary break from her 'surges', as she'd asked Jude and the midwife to call them, instead of 'contractions'.

'The birthing pool's all ready,' the midwife said a few minutes later when she reappeared in the delivery room, and they followed her through. Summer continued to be the picture of calm. She felt like a goddess, despite the power of the surges, but during the next examination she saw a frown on the midwife's face.

'You haven't progressed,' she said. 'I'm just going to get the doctor to have a look.'

Summer could feel a slight panic starting to grip her. She took Jude's hand.

'Don't worry,' he reassured her and, unless he'd suddenly become very good at acting, he really did look unruffled. 'It's all going to be fine.'

The doctor told Summer she could have another half an hour in the pool but that if there was no progression in that time they'd have to consider their options.

'Is the baby okay?' she asked.

'Yes, but we're concerned baby may start to get distressed if we wait too long. I'll be back in half an hour,' the woman said. She smiled. 'Good luck!'

But half an hour later it was clear that nothing had changed and, worryingly, the baby's heart rate indicated that it did appear to be in some distress.

'I'm afraid you're going to need an emergency C-section,' the doctor said, and Summer felt her panic increase as she was reminded of the twins' birth – the mad rush, the general anaesthetic and the blood transfusion.

'Keep breathing,' Jude said. 'You need to keep doing the breathing. It's going to be okay this time.' Summer looked at him and felt some of his composure rub off on her. Her hypno-birthing midwife had talked her through this possibility and she knew that staying calm was essential, even if she wasn't going to get the birth she'd hoped for.

'Can the consultant do one of those women-centred C-sections?' Summer asked, as she entered the theatre and hugged a cushion while the anaesthetist administered the epidural.

The doctor smiled. 'Yes, he can. Your midwife's just told me your history, but that was a long time ago. This experience will be different, I promise.'

She was right. Summer was able to see her baby being born as the drapes were lowered and she was immediately given skin-to-skin contact with her baby girl, although not for long as – being premature – she was whisked off to the Special Care Baby Unit almost immediately. But Summer realised as she was being stitched up that, as much as the birth hadn't been her dream plan, it had actually gone remarkably well. She hadn't needed a blood transfusion, and this time she'd seen her little baby make her entrance into the world.

'It didn't quite go according to plan,' she said to Jude, smiling ruefully.

'But it was still amazing! You were incredible. A goddess.' Summer smiled because that's exactly how she'd felt when she'd been in the water. And now, having battled her phobia and given birth, she felt just like a goddess all over again.

A little time later, Jude wheeled Summer along to the Special Care Baby Unit, where they finally got to meet their baby girl properly. She was in an incubator, all wired up, but looking completely adorable. Jude said she reminded him of a baby hedgehog, not realising Summer's father had given her the pet name of Hoglet as a newborn baby.

When Summer looked up at Jude from the incubator she saw him shed a tear and she knew right then that he'd meant it when he'd told her it wouldn't matter whether the baby was genetically his or not. To have been there when she came into the world was, it seemed, enough for him. He was a father. And as such, it seemed only fair to get his input on names.

'What shall we call her?' Summer asked him.

'It's up to you!' Jude said. 'You're her mum.'

'But you're her *dad*. And I want to know. If it was up to you, what would you name her?'

'Sabine,' he said, without hesitating. 'After my grandmother.'

Summer smiled. 'That's perfect,' she said. 'I couldn't have chosen better.' She looked at the tiny baby in the incubator, her fluffy dark hair sticking up in tufts. 'We'll call her Sabine Vita De Carteret.'

Chapter Forty-Four

Jersey, July

Jude

Unfortunately, being six weeks early, the baby was likely to be in the Special Care Baby Unit for some time. Summer sat by her side all day and most of the night with a look of pure longing on her face. She clearly ached to hold the baby to her breast.

'At least I can do this,' she told Jude, looking on the bright side when the unit gave her a breast pump and she started to express milk for the baby to receive via a feeding tube.

The first week was intensely stressful, but a couple of weeks on, Sabine was ready to graduate from the incubator to a cot, a huge deal in the world of the Special Care Baby Unit. It was only then that one of the doctors took Summer and Jude to one side to discuss an anomaly.

'Don't worry,' the doctor assured them, seeing their concerned faces. 'It's not a problem – it's just to let you know that we don't think Sabine was quite as premature as we first thought. Her progress has been so good we think she was probably four weeks early, rather than six. It doesn't make any difference – dating is always tricky. But it's good news, as it means Sabine is likely to be able to go home a bit earlier than you'd expected. You both look very relieved!' the doctor chuckled.

'It means more than you can imagine,' Summer said, smiling, then looking at Jude. The doctor returned her smile then moved on to the family at the neighbouring crib. 'You know what, Jude? You're a bloody saint to have taken on little Sabine not knowing whether you're her father or not, but I think that just about confirms it, don't you?'

'Two weeks makes a big difference,' Jude smiled, having done the necessary mental arithmetic. He picked Sabine up from her crib carefully, so that the wires that connected her to the heart monitor didn't tangle. 'I was never in any doubt,' he whispered to the baby in his arms.

Chapter Forty-Five

Jersey, November

The Naming Ceremony

'And could you tell me again who the guardians are?' asked Sally, the homely lady conducting the ceremony at the Atlantic Hotel. David and Beryl had made the journey from Australia for the occasion and were very excited, although they were a little disappointed it wasn't a proper christening. Jude had explained that Summer was the spiritual yet atheist child of hippies and – when it came down to it – she didn't want to be hypocritical.

'The beautiful Di – over there, sitting in the library tucking into the cream cakes. Jude's friend Eddie – just over there,' Summer said, pointing. 'And Sam, the girl with the peroxide-blonde hair standing next to the fish pond.'

'I *will* just need their surnames,' Sally said, and Summer realised she didn't actually know any of their last names.

'I'll just check,' she said, and she turned to Jude, who was chatting to the twins. They seemed – much to Summer's relief – to be taken with him. She handed Sabine over. 'Jude, she needs winding – do you mind?'

'Pleasure,' he said.

'And we need to tell Sally what the guardians' surnames are.'

'Eddie's is Thebault,' Jude confirmed. 'Not sure about Di or Sam though.'

'I'll check with Di, could you ask Sam?'

'Will do,' Jude replied, and he made his way to the indoor fish pond, gently rubbing Sabine's back as she slumbered on his shoulder.

'Hi, Sam,' he said, approaching her. She smiled back at him shyly.

'Jude, you're a natural,' she said.

'I'm not sure about that, but I love her to bits. Listen, we need your surname for the lady conducting the ceremony. I can't believe I don't know it!'

'Sure, it's Tremblay,' Sam said, taking a sip of champagne.

'No way! That's a coincidence – my surgeon in Canada was called Tremblay. Liam Tremblay. Do you know him? No, silly question – is it a really popular surname?'

'Actually, I do know him. He's my father.'

Jude looked at Sam, astonished. 'But . . . I mean – did you know he was the man who operated on me in Canada? What an incredible coincidence!' he laughed.

At this point, Daisy joined them. Sam shuffled uncomfortably. 'Daisy,' she said softly, 'I think it's time to come clean. Jude's just found out my surname. I've explained that my father was the surgeon who operated on him.'

'But what do you need to come clean about?' asked Jude.

Daisy looked up at him with a rueful grin. 'Do you remember saying to me, the day you told me about the brain tumour, that you didn't want to chase second opinions or drink disgusting juices or anything like that – you just wanted to enjoy the time you had left?' Daisy asked.

'Well, vaguely, yes. Why?'

'Sam explained to me, after you'd returned to Jersey, about her father's job. I knew you'd be unlikely to see him if I told you about him, so Sam told her dad all about you and, meanwhile, I rang your consultant again. Remember, you'd given me his contact details and waived your right to patient confidentiality so he could discuss your case with me? We put the two doctors in contact with each other and they agreed you were a good potential candidate to see Sam's father, though Mr Vibert said it would depend on the scan you were due to have that August so I was keeping all my fingers and toes crossed until then. I didn't want you to be scared off about it all so I asked the doctors to feign friendship. In fact, it wasn't really feigned in the end – they hit it off immediately. So that's how it all happened.'

Jude looked shocked. 'Dais, you're so naughty and way, way too clever! I can't believe it. And Sam, how can I ever thank you enough? You saved my life.'

'Nope,' she said humbly. 'That was Dad.'

Chapter Forty-Six

JERSEY, NOVEMBER

HILLTOP COTTAGE

Jude and Summer were still living nearby in Mandla, now with the baby in tow, though Sylvie had told them she'd be back to take up residence again before Christmas so they would soon need to put out feelers to find somewhere to rent, as Jude had long since given up the lease on his flat in town.

Di had been in wonderful form at the naming ceremony, but by the end of the day she'd looked tired. Sadly, her job as guardian to Sabine was short-lived. The following night, Di passed away in her sleep. Jude and Summer were deeply sad, especially as Prinny's health had started to decline as well, and, a week later, the vet advised them it was time to let him go.

When they said goodbye, Prinny proffered a paw to each of them, just as he had when they'd first met him at the animal shelter, and both Jude and Summer crumpled.

'Goodbye, old chap,' Jude whispered into his silky ear, inhaling the dog's scent for the last time. 'Thank you for sharing our journey with us. When I think about how it all began,' he said, looking up at Summer.

'I was living such a boring life, squandering every minute of it before I got ill. Then I met that old man in the hospital, then you, and Di, and Dennis, and your parents. And dear Prinny. I've got more out of life in the last eighteen months than I could ever have imagined.'

'You've been incredible,' Summer told him. 'And I think Prinny enjoyed coming along for the ride. Come on,' she said sadly. 'Let's not prolong the agony. It's time for us to go.' She gave Prinny one last hug and stood up, tears glittering in her eyes. 'Perhaps it was too much to ask for both of you to defy the odds.'

Arriving home from the vet's feeling despondent and yet needing to get on with the many tasks involved in caring for a young baby, Jude received a telephone call. He was staring sadly at the empty dog bed when his mobile began to ring.

'Hello?' he said.

'Mr De Carteret?'

'That's me.'

'Ah, jolly good. My name's Humphrey Blampied. I believe you knew my client, Di Smithson. I'm her solicitor.'

'That's right. She was my grandmother's best friend.'

'I think she might have considered you one of her best friends too. I'm dealing with her will. Di has left you her cottage.'

'Her cottage? But she lived in a home.'

'So that she could be cared for. But she never sold her main residence, which has gone to her children along with the rest of the estate, or the cottage. They've been kept in good repair.'

'But this must be a mistake. I'm not even family!'

'There's no mistake – I promise you. Would you like me to drop the keys off to you tomorrow? There will be a certain amount of paperwork to deal with but I imagine you might like to have a little look round?'

Jude could barely think straight but, 'Okay, yes please,' he said, and Mr Blampied promised to drop the keys off to him on his way to the office the following day.

◆ ◆ ◆

'I can't accept it,' Jude said to Summer the next day when they finally located the place – Hilltop Cottage – in Millais, just a few miles away from Mandla. It was in a rural spot not far from St George's church, with incredible sea views. There was a primary school just along the lane, too, which felt like a sign – perhaps Jude would finally return to teaching.

'Yes, you can,' replied Summer, who had a slumbering Sabine strapped to her chest. 'Jude, it's what Di wanted. And we're going to be homeless before Christmas. Oh Jude, just look at this place!'

It was a granite cottage, with a little pathway leading to it from a pale-green gate. To the side of the cottage was a vegetable patch and when they walked around to the back they found a surprisingly large garden with a children's swing hanging from a crab-apple tree.

Inside, it was tired but well maintained. A cosy sitting room to the left, with a granite fireplace and faded carpet and curtains. A dining room opposite, on the right, which Summer immediately earmarked as a playroom for Sabine. Then, at the back of the cottage, looking on to the garden, a large kitchen. The cottage dated back to the 1800s but the kitchen must have been new in the 1950s, by the look of it.

'We could update the kitchen . . .' Jude suggested.

'No,' whispered Summer. 'It's perfect,' she said, inspecting the Rayburn stove.

Upstairs there were three bedrooms, each with far-reaching sea views, and a spacious bathroom containing a well-worn yet perfectly useable white bathroom suite.

Their tour complete, Jude pulled the pale-green front door to. It shut with a comfortingly solid clunk. The winter sun was low in the sky and Summer sheltered her eyes from it as she took in the sweeping view of St Ouen's Bay below, the lighthouse gleaming.

'I told you the lighthouse wouldn't look any different in winter,' Summer said, smiling as she remembered a long-ago conversation they'd had.

'But it does,' Jude argued. 'It's whiter than ever in this light, and the sea's much steelier.' He sighed. 'I could never get bored of this view.'

'Are you going to keep the place?' Summer asked hopefully. 'Please say you are!'

'Yes,' Jude said eventually as he turned towards her and Sabine with a smile. 'It'll be ours. A place to be,' he said, mirroring Summer's words the very first time she'd visited his flat.

'A place to be together,' Summer finished. Jude looked at her, a new intensity in his eyes.

'I'm not prepared for this,' he began. 'I haven't got a ring or anything. But Summer, will you marry me? I mean, not quite yet, but once your divorce comes through . . . maybe in the spring?'

Jude watched Summer's face and saw the dimples spring to her cheeks as she smiled. 'There's nothing I'd love more,' she replied.

Epilogue

It was Christmas Eve and Summer was tucking Sabine up in her cot in the nursery. Jude had only finished decorating it a few days earlier – as soon as they'd moved in, the pair of them had set to giving the cottage a thorough 'scale and polish', as they called it, as if the house were just a rather old mouth in need of a bit of dental attention.

It meant Christmas had taken a bit of a back seat and the last few days had been spent in a frenzy of excitement as the pair of them rushed about with Sabine, buying a tree, lights, decorations, presents, wrapping paper and – of course – all the food and drink they'd need for the festive period. They'd expected to have a very quiet Christmas Day, just the three of them, but at the last minute they'd invited Cat and Eddie and their children, and Sylvie and Dennis, too. Then they'd received a message saying Vita and Frank were on their way, though it was getting late and there hadn't been any sign of them so far.

Satisfied that Sabine was drifting off, Summer crept stealthily towards the door. She could hear the rattle of pots and pans downstairs as Jude made a start on supper. She tiptoed across the landing into their bedroom and opened the window a little to try to lessen the powerful smell of fresh paint. Then she bent down and checked the box she'd kept hidden in the corner of the room since earlier in the afternoon. It was time to give Jude his gift. Summer picked up the box and carefully navigated the steep staircase, then deposited it in the sitting room, next to the fire. Jude had clearly just thrown another log on and it was blazing away, enveloping the room with its warmth and mellow light. Jude's television had been broken in the move, but the radio was playing gentle Christmas music and the slightly lopsided tree twinkled, adding to the cosiness of the scene and offering up that unmistakeable scent of Christmastime.

'Here,' said Jude, interrupting Summer's appreciation of the cosy sitting room. 'I've got you a drink,' he said. He was carrying a small tray loaded with two glasses of champagne and a bowl of nuts.

'Perfect timing,' Summer smiled, taking one of the glasses. 'I have a gift for you. An early Christmas present. Close your eyes.'

'But what if I'd rather wait until tomorrow?'

'It won't wait!' Summer laughed. 'Come on, close your eyes and put out your hands.'

Jude put down his glass and did as he was told, while Summer passed a small white ball of fluff into his arms.

'Gah!' Jude laughed. 'I wasn't expecting a living creature! Oh, it's beautiful. And so happy! Listen to it purring!' He looked thrilled.

'I'm so glad you're pleased. I know how much you loved Prinny, so I thought about another dog, but it just felt too raw. And as we've decided not to have any more kids, I thought we could give Sabine a pet sibling instead . . .'

'We can call her Santa Paws,' joked Jude.

'Actually, she already has a name . . . I got her from a farm down the road and the farmer's little girl had been calling her Snowdrop. I mean, we could change it . . .'

'No,' said Jude firmly. 'No, Snowdrop is perfect. Hey, listen . . . on the radio . . . Remember us listening to this song at Mandla exactly a year ago? "Have Yourself a Merry Little Christmas" . . .'

Summer listened and heard Judy Garland's dulcet tones comfortingly singing of troubles being overcome by the following year.

'It's true,' Summer mumbled as Jude pulled her towards him. 'What a difference a year makes . . . I mean, to think we might never have got back together, and then there was my phobia . . . I know we can't ever be complacent about our happiness, especially with everything you've been through health-wise. But somehow that makes what we have even more special.'

Summer looked up at Jude, about to kiss him, when the sound of something like a firework disturbed them.

'What the hell's that?' asked Jude, leaning towards the window to look outside. But Summer didn't need to look to know exactly what it was.

'The orange camper van,' she laughed. 'Frank and Vita. Of course. Just in time for the celebrations . . .'

Bibliography

A Doctor's Occupation: The dramatic true story of life in Nazi-occupied Jersey by John Lewis and John Nettles, Channel Island Publishing, new revised edition (July 2010)

The Hypnobirthing Book: An inspirational guide for a calm, confident, natural birth by Katharine Graves, Katharine Publishing, revised edition (2017)

Article from Ancestry.com re the 1911 Channel Islands census

Acknowledgments

Huge thanks, as ever, go to my incredibly supportive husband, Dan, my wonderful children – Ruby, Iris and Joey, my cats, my family and my friends (a special mention to Kate Mills for her invaluable assistance on the medical facts). My heartfelt gratitude also goes to Sammia Hamer (who has been so accommodating during the rather particular circumstances involved in editing this novel), Victoria Pepe, Melody Guy, Jenni Davis, Bekah Graham, Nicole Wagner and the rest of the Lake Union team. Finally, my thanks go to my loyal readers, whose on-going support and interest I truly appreciate.

About the author

Photo © 2015 by Charlotte Huish

Rebecca Boxall was born in 1977 in East Sussex, where she grew up in a bustling vicarage always filled with family, friends and parishioners. She now lives by the sea in Jersey with her husband, children and cats. She read English at the University of Warwick before training as a lawyer, and also studied Creative Writing with The Writers Bureau. *Christmas by the Lighthouse* is her fifth book. For the latest author updates, you can follow Rebecca at: www.rebeccaboxall.co.uk and www.facebook.com/christmasatthevicarage.

29025982R00139

Printed in Great Britain
by Amazon